MW01132645

Seriously
HAPPY

Seriously Happy © 2024 Quarto Publishing plc.
Text © 2024 Ben Aldridge.

First published in 2024 by Holler, an imprint of The Quarto Group.
100 Cummings Center, Suite 265D, Beverly, MA 01915, USA.
T +1 978-282-9590
www.Quarto.com

A CIP record for this book is available from the Library of Congress.

ISBN 978-0-7112-9780-7
EBook ISBN 978-0-7112-9781-4

Designer: Michelle Brackenborough
In-house Designer: Lyli Feng
Editor: Holly Edgar
Production Controller: Nikki Ingram
Art Director: Karissa Santos
Publisher: Debbie Foy

Printed by CPI UK 062024

9 8 7 6 5 4 3 2 1

The paper and board used in this book are made from wood from responsible sources.

Cover and interior illustrations: Michelle Brackenborough
Image credits: Olga S L/Shutterstock.com; RoseRodionova/Shutterstock.com

Seriously HAPPY

10 life-changing philosophy lessons from Stoicism to Zen to supercharge your mindset

BEN ALDRIDGE

For Oli and Helen

CONTENTS

Part 1
INTRODUCTION

"A JOURNEY
OF A THOUSAND
MILES BEGINS WITH
A SINGLE STEP."
LAO-TZU

What is Your "Happy"?

Everyone wants to be happy, right? But not everyone knows what they need to do to achieve this. We're told that we should be happy, but the road map to getting there isn't always clear. Of course, happiness is different for everyone.

It's important to figure out what "happiness" means for you.

Get this right, and it can have a profoundly positive impact on how you live.

In this book, we're going to look at ancient philosophies that can guide you toward a happier, more fulfilling life. These ideas, rooted in the wisdom of the past, offer valuable insights that are still relevant today. Although these philosophies are very old, they have stood the test of time. What worked for folks 2,000 years ago can also work for you today.

Human beings are still influenced by powerful emotions like fear, greed, anger, love, and joy. Being chased by a tiger would still scare the pants off you in the modern world, as it would have back in the day. Cultures and societies might have changed and evolved, but our brains are essentially the same, and emotional responses such as stress and anxiety arise as responses to everyday "threats" and challenges.

The ancient Greeks thought about happiness differently than we do today. Believe it or not, being happy ALL the time wasn't the main goal for a lot of these ancient philosophers. They were aiming for something a little different ... They were looking for a "good life" overall, a life that flowed well, irrespective of the ups and downs. The philosophers acknowledged that life isn't always easy, so having the strength of character to endure those difficulties was a must.

The word they used for happiness and living a good life was eudaemonia.

The ancient Greeks believed that the best way to achieve eudaemonia was through personal growth fostered by cultivating a virtuous character. The idea was that with a strong character and living well, happiness, contentment, and a balanced, chilled mind would follow. Sounds nice, right?

This idea is very different from the modern, often materialistic, and conditional approach to happiness. Ancient philosophers would have seen the mindset of "I'll be happy when I get a new pair of sneakers/when my exams are over/when I have thousands of followers on social media" as superficial because it bases happiness on external factors.

Ancient Greek philosophy sought out a type of happiness that came from personal growth and good character. This inner happiness was based on looking at the world in a certain way and cultivating a frame of mind that says,

"Whatever happens, we'll handle it."

The Eastern philosophical take on happiness was similar. In fact, many Eastern philosophies, like Taoism, Zen, and Buddhism, focus on training the mind and finding balance in life. By developing a strong mind, we will be better equipped to deal with the turbulence of life. It's fascinating that, although they developed thousands of miles apart, similar concepts surfaced within these different schools of philosophy.

So, my overall goal with this book is to introduce you to philosophical ideas that can help you build character. We'll be looking at how to grow resilience, increase focus, make better decisions, increase confidence, deal with difficult people, and much more.

And for the ancients, a good character comes with a delightful side order of serious happiness!

Seriously ... Anxious

Several years ago, I found myself in an incredibly dark and unhappy place, slipping into a pit of intense anxiety and panic attacks. I say slipping ... but it was more like being hit by a truck. I was so badly prepared for this. At the time, I didn't even know what anxiety was. It seemed to come out of the blue. Upon reflection, I can see why this happened to me. I'll explore this a little more later, but it was an accumulative effect of poor lifestyle choices and bad habits that fed my mind with negative content and a predisposition for anxiety. Not a great combination for a balanced life.

For those unfamiliar with anxiety, let me give you a very basic sense of what it can feel like. Imagine for a minute that you're about to jump out of a plane. You've signed up to do a skydive, and now it's crunch time. You are thousands of feet up in the air, the plane door is open, you've got an instructor strapped to your back, and there's one minute left until you jump. In this situation, you'd probably be feeling something in your body. Adrenaline would be racing through your veins, which would cause physical symptoms: shaky hands, a dry mouth, wobbly legs, nausea, sweaty palms, a racing heart, a sense of impending doom, shortness of breath, negative thought patterns, and a general feeling of overall panic.

All of this nervous energy is normal and expected in a skydiving situation. You're about to do something frightening, and adrenaline is your body's response to that stressful situation.

Make sense?

Now imagine that you're sitting on your sofa at home, and you suddenly feel like this ... Well, this is what happened to me. Out of context, adrenaline and fear are incredibly scary. When you can't pinpoint why you feel utterly petrified, your mind can start to freak out. I thought I was dying!

For me, the anxiety started one day, and that was it—wave after wave of intense panic and fear kept washing over me.

I felt like I was drowning. It was utterly exhausting. Any chance of happiness in my life seemed to be blocked by this overwhelming anxiety. The situation became so all-consuming that I found it hard to leave the house. I felt scared of everything and didn't know what might cause my next panic attack. It was a horrible place to be.

I desperately began seeking answers to understand what was happening to me. I needed to know how to fix myself and start feeling happy again. And I needed to know fast. I started with a visit to the doctor, who helped to clarify exactly what was going on with me (diagnosis: anxiety and panic attacks). This was a solid place to begin. However, I didn't feel like I wanted to follow the doctor's suggestion of talk therapy. I was uncomfortable talking about it, so I stubbornly decided to deal with the problem by myself. In hindsight, seeking professional help for my mental health concerns would have been the smarter move. These days, I would always recommend seeking professional help.

Thankfully, all of this didn't backfire, and my salvation came to me through books. Lots of books. I began using them as a way for me to understand and work through my anxiety.

During this period of intense reading, I discovered philosophy. This profoundly changed everything: it was my gateway into the world of philosophical ideas and self-improvement.

My journey started for real with Stoicism—an ancient Greek and Roman philosophy that is strikingly pragmatic.

I fell in love with the ideas and found them incredibly helpful in alleviating my anxiety. The more I read about the Stoics, the more engaged I became. When I think back on this time in my life, there are two main ways that Stoicism helped me:

- It allowed me to start understanding how my mind worked. Stoic philosophy is packed with ideas that I could try out in the real world. For example, it gave me suggestions on approaching difficult situations, navigating powerful emotions, and boosting my sense of gratitude.

- Stoicism encouraged me to start pushing myself out of my comfort zone. At first, this was doing small things like leaving the house, but over time it built up to more adventurous stuff like climbing alpine peaks. You see, the Stoics would deliberately seek out tough situations as a way to build a strong mind. This was their form of mental training. I thought this was fascinating, so I decided to start using it in my life. That's when things shifted—dramatically.

By seeking out these challenges, I began rebuilding my shattered self-trust. This helped me profoundly change my relationship with my anxiety. I started to feel in control of my mind again. After a while, I stopped having panic attacks and feeling permanently anxious. This was remarkable. Sure, it might have taken several months to get there, but I felt like color had returned to my life. I could finally breathe again. It was such a huge relief.

It felt like philosophy had saved me. In the process, my life went from small and scared to MUCH more adventurous. Thanks to Stoic philosophy, I found myself in many crazy situations: I took ice baths, hiked to mountain summits, ran marathons, climbed giant cliff faces, paddleboarded on choppy seas, swam outside in the winter, learned random new skills (like solving the Rubik's cube, stunt driving, folding origami, and picking locks), I ate a ton of strange food, completed long distance walks, visited countries all over the planet, slept in very unusual places, deliberately embarrassed myself in countless ways, forced myself to face my phobia of needles by getting acupuncture—and much more. Whenever I pushed myself with a new challenge, I got to try out more ideas from Stoicism. It was an exhilarating way to learn, and I feel incredibly lucky and grateful that I was able to do these things.

Alongside all of this, I began getting deeper into other philosophies and trying them out in my life. It was exciting but also extremely helpful. I loved discovering a new idea that I could take on an adventure with me. I would ask myself: "How could this aspect of the philosophy help me in the real world?"

The answers were usually practical and surprisingly easy to apply. I learned how to keep calm in frightening situations, make quick decisions on my feet, deal with difficult people, manage setbacks, and grow my confidence to no end. These are only a few of my most valuable lessons, but there are many more.

In the end, I began sharing my experiences with others—I felt that if I could at least help one person change their relationship with their anxiety and get into philosophy, then all of the effort would be worth it. So, I started writing books and talking to audiences around the world about these ideas. I haven't looked back, and I hope these ideas will help you, too.

The Problem & the Solution

In the modern world, we have a big problem—a lot of us aren't particularly happy. In fact, many of us are anxious, depressed, and struggling with day-to-day existence. It's almost as if we don't know how to live well.

Philosophy saved me, so I'm a little biased, but I think that some of our modern-day problems could be solved by people thinking more philosophically. I'm not suggesting that philosophy is the ONLY solution, but some of the ideas from it may be able to help.

Philosophy literally means "love of wisdom" in Greek. And that's really what it's all about—finding solid life advice that actually works. There are countless lessons for us to learn from these ideas.

Unfortunately, philosophy has gotten a bad rep over the years. It's hardly taught in schools these days and isn't pushed front and center in today's society. Many people assume that philosophy is dry and dusty, which doesn't help. I'm guilty of this.

When I used to think about philosophy, I would imagine stuffy libraries packed with boring tweed-jacket-wearing, pipe-smoking academics. I had this image of them droning on about uninspiring ancient men and women who weren't relevant to the modern world. What could someone so far removed from modern life possibly teach me? Well, it turns out that I was very wrong. We can learn a lot from these ancient thinkers. They are truly fascinating. And they profoundly changed my life in countless ways.

Feed the Right Wolf

There's a powerful story with roots in some Native American traditions that illustrates the importance of what we feed our minds with. This is the perfect way to highlight how bringing philosophy into our lives can help us.

The legend explains that there are two wolves in each of us—one good and one bad. The wolf that "wins" this internal battle is the wolf you choose to feed. For example, if you consume negativity, lean into anger, and dwell on hate, the bad wolf will grow bigger, but if you choose to feed the part of you that is loving, compassionate, and joyful, the good wolf will grow.

Similar to the two wolves, the philosophies in this book offer different paths to choose from. By focusing on positive ideas, we can cultivate a happier and more fulfilling life.

It's obvious which is the better choice. If you want to feel good, you need to feed that part of you. A diet of philosophy and memes should do the trick. Maybe the odd snack here and there. In all seriousness, what you consume really does matter. Be cautious about what you allow into your life. I made the mistake of focusing on fear and negativity all the time, and this led me to a deeply anxious and unhappy place. OK, it wasn't the only thing that made me anxious and unhappy, but it certainly fueled the fire.

Knowing how powerful the mind can be is super important. Your mind is your most valuable asset and will determine the quality of your life. It therefore makes sense to train the mind and be conscious of what you are feeding it. And THAT is where philosophy comes in. If we become what we mentally consume, filling up on helpful ideas that enable us to live a better life seems like pretty good medicine to me.

How to Use This Book

This is a very practical book—no, really! At the end of each chapter, there are several challenges for you to try so you can get to know the philosophies in a deeper way. This is how the philosophy will come to life and start changing your way of thinking and being.

Disclaimer: Some of the challenges are a little bizarre, so be prepared to do a few weird things in the name of self-improvement. When your friend witnesses you walk a 'pet banana' down the street, you'll have a little explaining to do ... More on this later.

We cover a lot of ground in these pages and will embark on a journey through various philosophical traditions from around the world, including China, Japan, India, Nepal, Greece, and Italy. The truth is, each of these philosophies could fill a whole book, but the aim here is to spark your curiosity and inspire you rather than give you a comprehensive guide to each one. I've had to be quite selective when choosing these philosophies, since there are just so many to explore. I'll therefore be sharing my favorite philosophies with you—these are the ones that have had the biggest impact on my life. I'll be introducing you to Stoicism,

Cynicism, Zen, Taoism, Buddhism, Epicureanism, Aristotelianism, and the Socratic School, with a focus on exploring specific ideas that you can use in your daily life. Ideas that hopefully can help you to thrive.

It's important to be mindful that these ancient philosophies are from very different times. They were formulated during an era when women weren't encouraged to share their thoughts and have a voice. Thankfully, some of these philosophies and philosophers inspired a more equal and open-minded perspective on the world and directly pushed back against a lot of social norms of the day. You'll meet some of these changemakers in this book. Nevertheless, the times still impacted the philosophies, which means they were developed in an era when men dominated philosophical discourse.

It's also worth noting that several of the philosophies we'll be exploring are both a philosophy and a religion—Zen, Taoism, and Buddhism, in particular. The line between religion and philosophy is nuanced, and a lot could be written about it. But for the purposes of this book, we will focus on the philosophical core of these practices and not their religious and ceremonial components.

And a final note before we dive in: all the ideas from the philosophies in this book will be compatible with whatever faith you already have in your life. So, don't feel that at any point I'll be trying to convince you to abandon your faith—or lack of faith, for that matter. This is simply a presentation of ideas.

OK, let's get going. Your character-building for happiness and eudaemonia starts now ...

Part 2
THE PHILOSOPHIES

Chapter 1

POWER UP
YOUR FOCUS

The Zen Philosophy

As I cautiously stepped onto the metal rung walkway, the wind carried a sense of isolation. Below, a vast expanse stretched out as I looked down ... The sheer drop seemed to go on forever. The rungs were spaced evenly and pinned to an overhanging cliff. They looked like giant staples, with one set for your hands and one set for your feet.

I took a deep breath and stepped over an airy gap to the next rung. It was about an inch thick, so only some of my foot was in contact with the metal. I gripped the handholds tightly and remained focused. I pushed on and clambered my way across the face of the cliff until I made it to a rocky path that wasn't so exposed. Phew. I caught my breath and looked back at the crazy climb ... It looked wild!

Snowcapped mountains and alpine trees framed the distant horizon, but in the thin air of the Colorado Rocky Mountains, it felt like Matt, my climbing buddy, and I were the only souls in that vast, remote place.

This particular via ferrata (essentially, iron ladders and steps bolted to the cliff) felt like a daring adventure! Via ferratas were created in the European Alps in the late 1800s but really took off during the World War I in the Italian Dolomites as a way for soldiers to travel around the mountains quickly. It's now a cool challenge for climbers to enjoy while having the relative safety features of ladders and wires to clip into (so that you don't fall off the cliff if you slip).

While climbing the route, there was no time for daydreaming; the scary drop below made sure of that. This FORCED me into the present moment and to FOCUS—this is one of the things I love about climbing and doing things that require care. Amid the heights and the breathtaking views, distractions disappear, and I'm left with just the moment. Pure experience. This is mindfulness and focus in action.

This heightened awareness, typical of extreme activities like climbing, made me think about life. The climb became a metaphor for facing challenges, making me wonder: Can we apply the same focus to our everyday lives? Not just extreme or highly engaging tasks. Are we able to handle distractions? Can we remain present when out walking in the park? Or while studying with the temptation of video games close by? Or lining up for something? Or waiting for friends?

If we can learn to focus our minds on what we are doing in the moment and live a more present existence, our favorite music will sound richer, our food will taste more delicious, and our time with friends will be more enjoyable.

In a world full of distractions—notifications, school, demands, and the constant buzz of life—finding your center becomes a modern-day superpower. It's a little like clinging to those iron rungs ... Only this time, it's with the chaos of life. Can you stay focused despite the onslaught of things pulling at your attention? Distractions are everywhere these days. And when we are distracted, it's hard to think clearly.

Living in a soup of whirling thoughts can be exhausting.

Enter the philosophy of Zen—a wonderful method for navigating the turbulence of being a teenager. It's like a tool to help you stay in the zone, whether you're facing a thrilling climb or just dealing with everyday drama. Through Zen, you can learn how to reclaim focus and live in the moment.

All About Zen

Zen is one of my favorite philosophies because it's very practical, and, at its core, there is an emphasis on being present and focused. A type of Buddhism, it originated in India around 500 BCE and later made its way to China. In China, Buddhism was adapted as it mixed with Chinese philosophies. At this time, it was known as Chan. The ideas eventually landed in Japan through cross-cultural exchanges with China. Here, they mixed with Japanese traditions, and Zen was born. The philosophy has now spread worldwide.

Zen (meaning "meditation") is about finding enlightenment, which, in simple terms, is the ability to think clearly, reduce mental suffering, and see the world without overanalysis or labels. In Zen, it is said that we can achieve clarity of thought or enlightenment through meditation. This is the foundation of the philosophy.

After enough meditation, there comes a point when the meditator has a sudden "enlightenment experience," which is a moment of deep understanding—a knowing of truths. This moment of deep realization about the nature of the universe and our place within it is called satori. In the Zen tradition, some wonderful (if sometimes a little bizarre) events have caused someone to have this immediate insight.

For instance, Mugai Nyodai, also known as Chiyono, was the first female Rinzai Zen master. In the mid-to-late 1200s, she established a Zen temple for women in Kyoto, Japan, and became an incredibly important figure within the philosophy. Her enlightenment story has become legendary within Zen.

Although Chiyono had meditated and studied for years, it was a very mundane experience that caused her to have a breakthrough and view the world differently. One night, Chiyono was carrying a bucket of water back to the temple. The moon was reflecting in the water when the bottom of the bucket suddenly broke, and the water poured out. The disappearance of the moon's reflection from her bucket triggered a profound moment of understanding for Chiyono, leading her to experience satori.

Or how about the intriguing story of Ohashi, a Japanese Buddhist nun who lived in Japan sometime in the 1800s? Despite her fear of lightning, she chose to meditate during a storm one night.

Lightning crashed onto the veranda, and Ohashi lost consciousness. When she woke up, she experienced satori and became enlightened. Disclaimer: this doesn't mean you should start chasing storms in the pursuit of enlightenment.

A seemingly random and simple experience to an observer might actually be the profound insight that the meditator has been searching for. They say, don't judge a book by its cover. Well, don't judge enlightenment by how random it is. Anything might cause a breakthrough.

Two Schools of Thought

Zen is typically split into two distinct schools: Rinzai and Soto.

Rinzai: This school focuses on using Zen koans, which are thought-provoking riddles designed to challenge conventional thinking. The koans aim to push you toward a more intuitive and direct experience of reality. Examples include questions like, "What is the sound of one hand clapping?" or "If a tree falls in the forest and no one is there to hear it, does it make a sound?" Zen students mull over koans deeply and, after considerable time, present their answers to their Zen master. Most of the time, the Zen master might say, "NOPE. Try again!" However, there are no right or wrong answers; rather, the emphasis is on whether the student grasps the deeper meaning of the koan and Zen philosophy as a whole.

Soto: This school focuses more on meditation. Students dedicate serious amounts of time to deep meditation, aiming to enhance their concentration and clarity of thought. The training can be rigorous and demanding, and students can spend days in silence, committed to the goal of enlightenment. The keisaku (a flat wooden stick) is sometimes employed to nudge students who aren't alert, focused, or awake.

Empty Temples & Busy Minds

Zen temples have a unique feeling of space and emptiness. They are uncluttered and clean. Japanese Zen gardens and temple grounds are also carefully crafted, creating spaces where you can sit and soak in the calm. There's a stillness that has a certain power, and simply sitting and looking at a Zen garden can be very peaceful.

When Zen students visit the temples (or move to the temples, if they fully commit to monk life), a big chunk of their time is spent meditating. One popular form is called "zazen," which means "seated meditation." Yes, it's exactly what it sounds like: sitting down, doing nothing, for quite a while. All you need is a cushion called a "zafu," and a gong or bell signals the start of a meditation session. Students do these sessions multiple times a day, and the morning kicks off with an early meditation session. Sometimes there's chanting, sometimes not. There are many different types of meditation, but zazen keeps it simple.

It's all about focusing on the breath. When your mind wanders off, you just bring it back to the breath.

This goes on and on until the session is over.

One of the main purposes of all this meditation is to help Zen students better appreciate the simple things in life:

- the sound of a boiling teakettle
- raindrops on windows
- falling leaves
- the sound of a frog jumping into a pond
- a sharp and cold night in the heart of winter
- breath swirling in the air
- fog
- dappled sunlight
- puddles
- salt and vinegar potato chips (in my case).

This is often the inspiration for a lot of Zen poetry. OK, maybe not the potato chips ...

A huge amount of scientific research has been conducted to show how meditation can alter the brain in an observable way. A lot of it is based on getting hardcore meditators like monks and then scanning their brains while they meditate or do various tasks. It has been shown that their brains operate differently from those who have never meditated. They pretty much have superpowers. Well, almost.

In one recent study documented in the National Library of Medicine database, scientists observed an increase in gray matter on MRI brain scans after subjects undertook a course in meditation training. Gray matter is a crucial part of the brain that contains nerve cell bodies, and it plays a vital role in various functions, such as muscle control and sensory perception, including seeing and hearing. An increase in gray matter is often associated with positive changes in cognitive abilities, memory, and overall brain health. So, meditation literally changed the structure of the subjects' brains in a visible way. Incredible.

THERE'S A HAIR IN MY INK

Zen philosophy is filled with a whole host of quirky characters. There is a legend about a Zen monk who lived around 1000 CE and used to paint in a unique way. He would dunk his long hair in ink, splash it all over a blank canvas and then use the mess as the starting point for his pictures. The monk would then pick out patterns and images from the ink-splotch chaos by getting into a focused state of creativity.

On a separate note, look up some Zen ink paintings when you get a minute. Zen artists create beautiful pictures based on nature and the changing seasons. They often make great use of blank space, punctuating it with intricate brushstrokes.

The Music of the Universe

Zen has influenced many people—and not just Zen monks. One of my favorite contemporary examples is from the American composer John Cage (1912–1992). Deeply immersed in Zen Buddhism, he frequently meditated, hung out with Zen masters, and loved the philosophy. His most famous piece, 4'33", was directly inspired by Zen. The piece of music is pure silence ... nothing is played ... zilch ... no notes. The whole orchestra sits on stage and does nothing for 4 minutes and 33 seconds. The conductor comes out on the stage, waves their arms about, and then everyone is silent. There can be thousands of people sitting in the audience watching a performance ... all silent.

Cage was crafty because he was guiding his audience into a meditative state (without many of them realizing it). As they sat, absorbed in the moment, they would intensely listen to the ambient sound around them. Each performance brought something different—perhaps the air-conditioning unit might be buzzing in one venue, a cough barking in another. With these tiny variations in each recital, Cage skillfully encouraged people to tune in and listen to the music of the universe.

Cage would also listen intently to the traffic outside his window. He believed there was something profound about listening to the beeps, revs, and break squeaks. He said that Mozart and other composers would always sound the same, but traffic was unpredictable and random. What an interesting way of thinking about things!

Zen is a rich philosophy, offering many practical and insightful ideas on mindfulness, simplicity, and the profound interplay between the self and the universe. Though we've just scratched the surface here, these insights aim to kindle your interest and guide you toward the profound wisdom that Zen has to offer.

Seriously Happy Hack

Learning to meditate is a great place to begin if you want to cultivate focus. This will be a wise investment of your time and can help you increase your attention span, develop mindfulness, and calm your overthinking.

Becoming more Zen starts when you give yourself the time and space to sit and do nothing.

The Challenges

These challenges based on Zen will help you connect to the philosophy and build your focus. They're great for stress management and becoming more present in your life. They may even upgrade your study sessions. These ideas come to life when you test them in the real world, so give them a try. I hope they help you find calm.

1   Sit Down, Shut Up

Getting into meditation will rewire your brain, and you will become calmer and more in control of your thinking. You will be better able to handle your emotions and become more focused. The great news is that you don't need to go to a temple for any of this to work—a simple commitment to a few minutes of quiet meditation each day can profoundly change the structure of your mind. Here's a simple outline for having a try:

1. Find somewhere quiet where you won't be interrupted. Get comfortable. You can sit or lie down, but if you choose to sit, try to keep your back straight. In Zen schools, they are VERY strict about sitting correctly. Soften your gaze, and relax.

2. Focus on your breathing, and observe it. Keep your attention here, and notice how it feels.

3. When you get distracted (which will happen), bring your attention back to your breath.

4. Repeat this for 10, 20, or 30 minutes. If this feels too daunting, start with 5 minutes and build up over time. You can set a timer so you don't have to worry about watching the clock.

If you've never meditated before, the first thing you will likely notice is how busy your mind is. The thoughts will keep coming. Wow—they can be unrelenting!

"What am I having for lunch? A bagel and cream cheese? No, I don't feel like it! Maybe soup. Oh, wait a minute—what did I need to do for Sarah? She wanted to borrow that book. Ahh, I must remember to find it. But didn't I lend it to Joe... Wait a second ... What day is it? ... OK ... Must ... Focus ..."

This is the battle that every meditator must face. Trust me, I've been there. I really struggled when I first started meditating. This is normal. In time, you will get better at letting thoughts float by like clouds. You can then become detached from your thinking and be the observer of your thoughts. Try doing it consistently for a few weeks, since it can take a little while to feel the impact.

2 The 4'33" Project

This challenge is based on John Cage's piece of silent music. It's very simple to perform. You don't even need an instrument.

Simply set a timer for 4 minutes 33 seconds, and listen to your environment. Notice how each performance is different every time.

Try this challenge in various places—downtown, by water, at home, in nature, in a busy café, or on public transportation. Notice the sounds around you, and follow them closely with your attention. Your eyes can either be open or closed—you decide.

After completing the challenge, you can look online and watch a performance in front of a live audience. Or even better, organize your own public recital!

3   A Moving Meditation

During long meditation sessions, Zen monks are encouraged to have a break by doing a walking meditation (after all, sitting down for long periods can be painful). They often walk around the room in a circle for this "break." I know it doesn't sound that exciting, but stay with me ...

This type of meditation feels distinctly different from sitting meditation, and it's a great way to bring meditation into your day. Let's face it: there are plenty of times throughout the day when you have to travel somewhere, so why not use them as a time to practice? It will help you improve your concentration and focus.

This will work for any type of movement, not just walking. And it's straightforward to do:

❋ Go out or stay in. Whatever you feel like.

❋ Slow your pace.

❋ Focus on your breathing and the feeling of moving through open space.

❋ Notice the sounds, sights, and smells around you.

❋ When you get distracted, bring your attention back to your breath and the sensation of movement.

❋ Repeat until the end of your trip.

Chapter 2

BECOME
SERIOUSLY
CONFIDENT

The Cynics

When I first began to experience anxiety, I lost all my confidence pretty much overnight. Panic attacks shattered my self-belief, and it felt as though I couldn't rely on myself to do anything. I felt mentally weak and useless—it was a tough time. I had to build myself back up from scratch.

My confidence only started to come back when I began pushing myself out of my comfort zone.

At first, it was with small things that I'd previously taken for granted, like catching the bus or the train, getting myself to work—that kind of thing. Simple daily stuff became overwhelming, and I had to force myself to do it. This pushing felt counterintuitive at the time, but it genuinely worked. When I got through something difficult, like buying myself a coffee or walking through a crowded shopping mall, it boosted my confidence and self-belief. This cycle of pushing myself through discomfort had a powerful effect on my mindset day by day.

Despite my past struggles with self-belief, I now speak in public as part of my job, and I honestly get a kick out of it. I talk to audiences around the world about philosophy, adventure, and mental health challenges. My last gig was delivering a keynote speech to 2,000 people in a massive concert hall. It was incredible; I felt confident and enjoyed every minute. However, it hasn't always been this way. Gaining the confidence to walk onto a stage and face a huge audience took time and effort.

I've had to work hard to challenge this crippling sense of anxiety.

Like most people, the thought of speaking in public terrified me at first. Glossophobia—the fear of speaking in public—ranks higher than death in a poll of common fears. Yes, you heard that right: higher than death. One of my first experiences of public speaking (or simply speaking UP in public!) was a total disaster. I went along to a talk by a famous explorer who shared incredible stories of polar bear encounters and expeditions through arctic storms. During the Q&A session at the end, I nervously raised my hand to ask a question. It was a small room with about 20 people, and everyone seemed friendly, but I could feel my heart thudding and my palms prickling with sweat. When it was my turn, I froze and struggled even to stutter out the word "expedition." The explorer had to finish my sentence for me. Frankly, it was cringeworthy ...

but the difference in my confidence between then and now is extraordinary.

It's ironic that, at one point, I struggled to ask a simple question in public, but now, speaking in public is part of my job. It just goes to show what can happen when you decide to leave your comfort zone and start facing your fears. I managed to change my mindset and learn genuine self-belief through consistently challenging myself to get on that stage and push through my discomfort.

Grow Your Confidence

Confidence is pretty awesome but is often misunderstood. Some think it means:

- being loud and extroverted
- taking charge of a room
- dominating conversations and "talking the talk."

But that's *not* always a sign of true confidence.

Confidence is knowing that you can handle whatever comes your way.

It means being ready to tackle the challenges that are thrown at you. Sure, you might struggle with them, but you can dive right in and give them your all. This inner trust and confidence will help you when you step outside of your comfort zone. Whatever you want to do in life, having the confidence to believe in yourself will empower you to do amazing things.

And guess what? Drumroll, please ... You don't have to be born confident because you can develop confidence and self-belief just like any other skill. And the best part? It can be a lot of fun. Sure, it takes some effort, but the rewards are totally worth it. The goal is to learn how to be cool with being uncomfortable. And that's where ancient philosophy comes in for inspiration. So, buckle up because we're about to jump in ...

Who Were the Cynic Philosophers?

In Athens, Greece, around 400 BCE, there was a group of ancient folk (Greek philosophers) whose approach to life can really help us cultivate confidence and self-belief. They were known as the Cynics, and their school of philosophy was called Cynicism.

The word cynic or cynical has a different vibe nowadays and didn't always have a negative meaning. The word cynic comes from the Greek word "kynikos," meaning "doglike." No, don't go—stick with me! "Cynic" was originally used in a derogatory way to talk about those who practiced this philosophy—probably because it reflected their wild and "rough" nature. Woof. This will become clear as we explore how the Cynics spent their time. Cynicism was all about questioning how we live our lives. It meant diving into freedom of speech, learning self-control, dealing with uncomfortable situations, and mental training for inner strength. (If you want to impress your pals, the Greek word for inner strength training is "askesis.")

The Cynics believed in preparing for all of life's challenges. So, they trained. And trained. They also believed in living an ascetic life—free from wealth and material comforts, which meant that some of the things they did would seem a little well ... strange. For example, they would:

- hug icy-cold statues in the winter, while naked
- roll around in boiling-hot sand in the summer
- sleep on a hard floor without a mattress or pillows
- walk barefoot and sometimes backward into crowds (on purpose).

All these challenges were part of their strategy to toughen up their minds and boost their confidence. And boy, did they love challenges. The more mentally demanding, the better.

Who Let the Diogenes Out?

There was one very famous Cynic named Diogenes. He was one of the creators of Cynicism and was nicknamed "the Dog" due to his rough-and-ready lifestyle. He also took his askesis to the extreme.

Let me paint you a picture to give you an insight into the mind of Diogenes and the Cynics. It's a lively Saturday afternoon in the Agora, Athens' bustling marketplace. Families are buying provisions and chatting with friends, and then ...

Diogenes strolls in, dragging his empty pet jar on a string—as if he's walking a dog.

Why? He did this on purpose to feel embarrassed, which was all part of overcoming that feeling in his mind.

Diogenes was in top physical condition and looked like an Olympic athlete. However, he was a little disheveled; he didn't own anything, and his home was a barrel in the heart of Athens. Don't feel too bad for him, though; all of this was out of choice—a way to live his philosophy. This minimalistic lifestyle allowed him to practice his Cynic ideas every single day. Overcoming the daily adversity of living in such a meager way became his askesis, or inner strength training.

Diogenes constantly challenged himself to do things that he found difficult. For example, the thought of eating raw meat made him feel queasy and nauseous. So, he did what any self-respecting, raw flesh-abhorring citizen would do and chomped down on a helping of raw octopus.

When asked what he got out of the Cynic philosophy, Diogenes said:

"If nothing else, I'm prepared for whatever happens."

He was also known to fart, burp, and even, um, *relieve* himself in public. When nature called, Diogenes answered. The people of Athens thought that Diogenes was bizarre, but he did these things to rebel against the rules of Athens. He wanted to make people question those rules and reflect on how they were living. The Cynics saw embarrassment as a way to train their minds; every time they faced a difficult situation, it made them mentally stronger.

PET BANANAS AND BANISHING SHAME

Diogenes walking his "pet jar" in the Athens marketplace has inspired modern psychology, and today there is a famous challenge called "the Banana Walk." It might sound odd, but this is done to help build confidence and bravery—and like it sounds, you tie a piece of string to a banana and walk it through a busy public place. Confession time ... I've walked all manner of fruit and vegetables in major towns and cities worldwide and can confirm that it's very embarrassing. But the genius of it was that it helped me to stop caring so much about what others thought.

The idea of "the Banana Walk" was originally created by Albert Ellis, the founder of a modern therapy called REBT (Rational Emotive Behavior Therapy) which helps people who lack self-confidence gain trust in themselves. It also helps them to overcome the fear of being judged by others.

Ellis expanded this further to create the challenge of "shame attacking." The idea is that by deliberately exposing ourselves to embarrassing situations, we can become desensitized to them. And therefore don't get embarrassed so easily. His own personal shame-attacking exercises included announcing the next stop on the train or bus out loud or singing at the top of his lungs while walking down the street. The idea has become more popular over time, and there are now "shame-attacking championships" where people come up with quirky ways to embarrass themselves.

Diogenes became so popular for his straight-talking wisdom that people would seek him out to learn from him. And although his ideas might have been radical, people were enthralled by what he had to say. An old story goes that Alexander the Great had a hankering to meet Diogenes. When he found Diogenes lying in the sun (soaking up the rays was an essential Cynic practice—mainly because it was free and felt good), he laid it on thick about how incredible and amazing he thought Diogenes was. He asked Diogenes if there was anything he could do for him. Being as powerful as he was meant that Alexander could grant any of Diogenes' wishes. The story goes that Diogenes replied, "Yeah, you can help me by getting out of the way. You're blocking my sun."

That statement could have gotten him killed (luckily, it didn't), but Diogenes didn't care about authority. He believed that respect was earned, not just granted because of circumstances. The fact that he lived a life outside of the norm meant that he could criticize society from an outsider's perspective. He wasn't afraid of losing his job or reputation, because he had nothing to lose. He believed in the ability to ask difficult questions and claimed that the most beautiful thing in the world is the freedom of speech.

The Rebel of Maroneia

Hipparchia of Maroneia was another famous Cynic who lived in Athens around the same time as Diogenes. She gained a reputation for her philosophical living when she adopted the Cynic lifestyle and chose to live a life of poverty on the streets of Athens. In the latter years of her life, Hipparchia became head of the Cynic school. Unfortunately, all her philosophical writings have been lost, but the insights that we have about her life are fascinating ...

At that time in Athens, societal norms discouraged women from attending public events and debates. However, the rebellious Hipparchia not only secured invitations, but once there, she would throw herself into the discussions with gusto. Her actions paved the way for future female philosophers to challenge the misogynistic beliefs of the day.

Hipparchia also encouraged her two children to live the Cynic way. She believed in mental toughness training, such as bathing them in cold water, offering them simple food (not too little, but not too much), and rocking them to sleep in an old tortoise shell rather than using a traditional cot. Her approach to life was considered extreme by many in Athens' society, but her behavior was revolutionary. She chose to live in a way that was true to her, even though many didn't think she could or should. This was self-belief and confidence in full swing.

So, maybe we aren't bathing in freezing cold water or lulling ourselves to sleep in tortoise shells, but Hipparchia's example of action over words and her unrelenting questioning mind inspire all of us.

The Cynics' way of seeing the world and their approach to building confidence, inner strength, and happiness were highly practical. Every time you step outside of your comfort zone and do something that makes you uncomfortable, you become mentally stronger.

The Challenges

If the thought of hugging an icy-cold statue doesn't appeal, but you'd like to exit your comfort zone like Diogenes or challenge the rules like Hipparchia, here are some Cynic philosophy-based exercises. These will help build your confidence and self-belief, and perhaps even help to make you seriously happy!

1 Take a Banana for a Walk

As mentioned earlier, inspired by Diogenes, I've walked bananas in London and carrots in Paris, and handed out leeks on a string at many of my public talks. You may be too afraid to walk a fruit or vegetable around town, but it's a fantastic way to boost your bravery and confidence. The day I first took a banana for a walk in a packed shopping mall in London was nothing short of mortifying. I thought how ridiculous the situation must look to passersby, but I took a deep breath and began weaving through crowds of shoppers. Yes, people looked at me. Yes, I felt sweaty and self-conscious throughout. But I survived. The second time, it was easier. The third time, no real worries. Turns out—the more you embarrass yourself, the easier it gets. Who knew?

2   Embarrassed, Moi?

As we know, the Cynics were keen on deliberately embarrassing themselves. So far, so cringe. And let's be honest, there are many times we do embarrass ourselves—but most of the time it's not intentional. Like the time I stacked it in a busy supermarket because I was hanging off the back of a shopping cart like a 7-year-old, causing it to shoot out from under me. There was a gasp from shoppers around me who could have stepped over me to reach the melons, but alas, they wanted to make sure I was OK, which made the whole experience even more embarrassing. This experience aside, believe it or not, we can gain from intentionally seeking out embarrassing situations. Read on ...

For this challenge, it's very simple: you should aim to embarrass yourself. On purpose. Now, there are many ways that you can do this, and I'd encourage you to be creative here. Go for something you think is embarrassing (I'm not you, so I don't know exactly what would embarrass you). Play around with ideas, and see what you can come up with. Obviously, don't do anything dangerous, offensive, or that might land you in trouble. And, side note: taking a friend along for the ride makes for some funny experiences and memories.

While "attacking your shame" with this challenge, I suggest that you pay attention to how it feels when you're embarrassed. Learn to sit with the discomfort in your body. Learn to let go. The more you do it, the easier it gets. This will help you feel comfortable in your own skin whenever all eyes are on you. With a little luck, it will also make you harder to embarrass.

3 Facing Your Fears

Facing things that you think are scary and learning to trust yourself in the process is POWERFUL. Most of us will avoid doing stuff that scares us like the plague, but like the Cynics, you can build confidence and be ready for any situation by challenging yourself to do stuff that you find a little, well, scary. Nothing dangerous, of course. We're not talking bear-wrestling or scaling a mountain in swimwear, but something that you find frightening but is also safe.

This fear challenge is based on a psychological practice called "fear exposure"—a practical method that helps people work through fears and phobias by slowly exposing them to things that scare them. It starts with small exposure, but over time, the exposure increases. If you're afraid of snakes, you'll start by looking at pictures of them. Then maybe looking at one in real life. Then, under the right circumstances (and with the right professional help, of course) you could work up to holding one. This method has helped millions of people work through a whole range of fears—from flying to spiders to swimming in deep water.

For example, if you fear heights, you might challenge yourself to take a lesson under professional guidance at your local climbing wall. You could then work up to a treetop adventure at an activity center or visit an observation deck in a tall skyscraper.

If you're scared of speaking in public, nominate yourself to perform or speak in front of your class. Practice ahead of time by speaking to a trusted friend or family member.

A technique called box breathing can help to calm you, too. It goes like this:

❋ *breathe in for a beat of 4*
❋ *hold for 4*
❋ *breathe out for 4*
❋ *then hold again for 4.*

Try to imagine a square where each side is worth 4 beats to help you visualize the exercise.

This happy hack helps to relax the body, which then helps relax the mind. 😌

Embracing your fears will see your confidence grow.

Chapter 3

BOOST YOUR CRITICAL THINKING

The Socratic School

Before I got into philosophy, doing mundane stuff like washing dishes was a chore. After diving into philosophy, washing bowls, plates, and silverware became an opportunity for me to train and exercise my mind. It's still not the highlight of my day, but I view it slightly differently. Philosophy has significantly altered my thought process; now, questioning my habits, thought patterns, beliefs, and assumptions is a routine part of life. In a way, my entire attitude has changed, and I'm much more open to new ideas. I love discovering a different perspective and really enjoy contemplating an unfamiliar take.

The biggest shift has been embracing critical thinking. To think critically, we don't need to remember a ton of random facts. We don't need to be intellectually gifted and able to solve complex equations. And we don't need countless years of higher education ... Phew! What we do need, though, is a system of thinking, a method that we can apply to everything life throws our way. And yes, I've got a great system to share with you in this chapter.

Critical thinking is about being objective. To think freely and critically, we need to look at all the facts available and build a position based on these. And when more facts come along, we update our thinking. It's scientific in its manner but without the lab coat. We can never be 100 percent certain all of the time. For now, we're good. Tomorrow? Well, let's see. Science is not set in stone; it's about staying adaptable and ready for change. If someone claims that science is "settled" on something, it should cause alarm bells to go off in your head.

While we can build an understanding with our current knowledge about something, this knowledge is precarious. The introduction of a minuscule piece of new information could easily overturn it. For example, I don't think purple swans exist, but if I started seeing them at the local pond, I'd have to rethink things a little in order to get to the bottom of what was happening. Is it a new species? Have my eyes stopped working? Is someone having fun with paint?

Those who refuse to update their worldview when presented with new facts are not critical thinkers. We would therefore be wise to hold our opinions lightly—as if they were delicate glass ornaments.

Human knowledge is constantly progressing as we discover new ideas that challenge us. If you want an example of this, just look into the wonderful world of quantum physics. There are some truly bizarre discoveries here that are disrupting our entire understanding of the universe. For instance, quantum entanglement, described by Einstein as "spooky action at a distance," challenges our understanding of connection by showcasing that two objects can remain intricately linked despite being separated by huge distances—this has been shown in various experiments and challenges our thinking about how we connect to each other and to the world around us. And this is just one area of scientific research. New revelations are coming in thick and fast! Quantum physics is a massive wormhole for you to explore if you want to expand your mind further.

To think critically, we must not "settle" on anything. We must endeavor to ask questions about the world around us. We must always ask difficult questions, and we must not stop asking them.

These questions can help us better understand our place in the universe. They can also help us become better problem solvers, stronger decision-makers, and more open-minded folk. We can learn from the Greek philosopher Socrates how to question absolutely everything. This is the foundation of critical thinking.

The Big Daddy of Western Philosophy

Socrates is the heavyweight philosopher of ancient Greece. He revolutionized thinking around the world and inspired countless people to set up their own schools of philosophy. In fact, he's considered to be so important that any Greek philosopher who was around before him is now known as pre-Socratic. He was kind of a big deal.

Socrates was born in Athens in 469 BCE and spent most of his life in the city. As a boy, he was keen on learning and studied a mix of philosophy and rhetoric. He later served as a soldier in the army and was deployed in battles during the Peloponnesian War. He gained a reputation for being courageous and having great endurance during this time. After this chunk of his life, he became the philosopher and teacher we all know and love—well, the youth of Athens certainly thought that! Socrates was unconventional for the time—he didn't wash, wore his hair long, and walked around barefoot. His bulging eyes and stubby nose were prominent features that many people commented on when writing about him. He became known for his method of questioning absolutely everything—literally everything: the nature of reality, the way society worked, and the afterlife ... No stone was left unturned. He gained the nickname "the gadfly" because he kept asking questions while debating.

His method was unrelenting, like a fly that keeps buzzing around you on a hot day. Socrates would keep coming back for more.

Notably, he left no written records of his teachings, relying on the oral tradition and embodying his philosophy in his way of life. The only accounts we have of Socrates are from others. This naturally means that the picture we build of him is influenced by how those people saw him. Our two main sources are his most famous student, Plato, and another (not-so-famous-by-comparison philosopher) called Xenophon. They've both written about Socrates and have created slightly different characters in their books. At the core, we still have the same Socrates—the man who would question everything. But there are a few subtle differences in how they wrote about him. For instance, Plato's version of Socrates tended to ask more questions, whereas Xenophon's Socrates used to offer up opinions more frequently.

Socrates was sentenced to death by the Athenian court in his early seventies for "corrupting the youth" and having "incorrect" views. Basically, he was encouraging younger generations to ask questions and inspiring critical thinking. This is all very sketchy and when you dig into it, it's pretty clear that Socrates had upset people in power with his continuous questioning. He was openly critical of the societal structure in Athens and several of its prominent citizens, which was likely the main reason for his death sentence. Those in power wanted him gone.

In Plato's book *The Apology*, we learn about Socrates' trial. It's an interesting read and a detailed account of Socrates standing up in court to defend himself against his accusers. It's hard to read it and not be on Socrates' side. The poor guy was clearly set up. After being found guilty, he was forced to drink a cup of hemlock (poison), which he did without resistance.

The Socratic Method

Socrates had a methodical approach to his philosophy that was very much based on critical thinking. Nowadays, it's known as the Socratic Method. It has the following features:

- **Questions:** Socrates believed that constantly asking questions would help us understand the world around us. Many of these were open-ended and acted as a way of driving his philosophical inquiry.

- **Conversation:** A back-and-forth exchange of ideas between people would allow a more profound understanding of the topic under discussion. The combination of different points of view was powerful.

- **Cross-examination:** This helps to highlight what makes and does not make sense by uncovering contradictions, assumptions, and inconsistencies in beliefs or arguments.

Socrates traveled around Athens to roast people using this method. He would often get people tied up in their own thinking until they were confused and began to question themselves deeply. His style of interrogation could be sneaky and unrelenting. He would get a person to state their position on a subject and then find contradictions within their thinking. Realizing that they held two contrasting opinions on a topic would cause that person's position (and often their credibility) to collapse instantly.

For example, one person says they hate nuts, yet they love almond milk lattes with hazelnut shavings served in a mug shaped like a giant nut. Another swears they only eat healthy food but have milk chocolate all over their face and chip crumbs on their T-shirt.

This method or concept of finding and highlighting inconsistencies in someone's thinking is also called an "elenchus." Most people, faced with their own inconsistencies, may find it challenging to hold their position as they struggle to justify themselves. The only way they can get out of this situation is to admit that they are wrong and update their thinking (which is critical thinking in action). Bravo to them if they are adaptable enough to do this. On the other hand, some people struggle, unwilling to admit they are wrong. They may even pretend that they didn't really think like that in the first place ... Yeah, these people aren't fans of the elenchus.

Significant Women

So, where did Socrates get his wisdom from? Well, it came from a variety of places. Much of it came from simply paying attention to the answers he received from his incessant questioning, but some came directly from other philosophers.

One of Socrates' most notable teachers was the Greek philosopher and

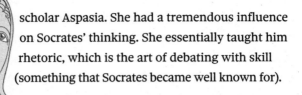

scholar Aspasia. She had a tremendous influence on Socrates' thinking. She essentially taught him rhetoric, which is the art of debating with skill (something that Socrates became well known for).

Aspasia managed to avoid the many restrictions imposed on women within Athens at the time that limited their involvement with public life. She circumvented these rules, since she technically wasn't a resident of the city. She knew what she was doing and was able to set up an academy. Here, she taught the elite women of Athens how to live well and flourish in society. It's worth noting that her teachings weren't just for the upper classes, since she clearly inspired many other movers and shakers in the city with her thoughts and ideas. Aspasia's public lectures would draw in many influential people.

In *Symposium*, a famous book by the Greek philosopher Plato, we learn about Socrates' views on love. If you get the chance to read it, do: it's a short book about a bunch of guys drinking at a social gathering and talking about love. Each attendee is asked to give a speech about love. Socrates drops a whale of a speech where he explains how love can help elevate the human mind in its quest for knowledge and understanding—and he credits a woman named Diotima as being the source of his knowledge on this topic. Now, Diotima clearly had a significant impact on his thinking, but she is kind of an enigma, and we don't know much else about her. She may well be a fictitious character created by Plato for this book (potentially inspired by Aspasia). Still, she has managed to become an important figure in philosophy. The fact that Socrates makes a point of crediting her with teaching him everything he knows about love shows respect and appreciation for the female perspective—a view that wasn't widely held in ancient Athens. When Plato's book *Symposium* came out around 385 BCE, it framed a female as the height of wisdom and insight, which would have been revolutionary at the time. This shows how vital philosophy has been in challenging narratives within society.

TAKING IT TOO FAR?

So many philosophical schools were inspired by Socrates' unrelenting questioning of the world around him. In fact, a school called the Skeptics took this questioning to the next level. They used rigorous doubt and scepticism as the basis for their entire philosophy. Some feel that they went a little too far. You decide ...

The father of Greek Skeptism was named Pyrrho (he was also the most extreme Skeptic of all time). Pyrrho questioned absolutely everything, including the reliability of his own senses—since he genuinely didn't think even they could be trusted. His scepticism extended to such a degree that stories still circulate about his students having to stop him from walking off cliff edges and into busy roads. Why? Because he wouldn't listen to his senses. Ever.

Is that rabid dog barking at me because it wants to bite me? Or does it want to hang out? Only one way to find out ... Pyrrho, NO ... ! He was lucky enough to have such great friends, since legend goes that they kept him from walking into lots of unfortunate situations and accidents over the years.

Around a similar time to Socrates, a philosopher in West Africa named Orunmila was also profoundly impacting society—and we can draw many parallels between these two figures. Orunmila was reportedly born around 500 BCE in Nigeria, where he had a significant influence on the life and culture of the Yoruba people. Some see him as a historical figure, others as a sage, but he is also called an "inter-dimensional being" and an "orisha" (a deity). There are myths and legends all around Orunmila, and we can't be entirely sure about the details of his life. However, we do know that he is integral to the Ifa religion and is known for his wisdom, knowledge, and guidance—often through divination practices still used by Ifa priests today.

The Nigerian philosopher Sophie Olúwolé pointed out a striking resemblance between Orunmila and Socrates. Her work explores how both of these historical figures had remarkably similar ideas.

Both emphasized cultivating virtue and leaning into critical thinking. They didn't believe that material possessions were the be-all and end-all of life—in fact, the pursuit of wisdom and virtuous living was seen as a better use of time.

There are also similarities in their teaching style. Neither of them actually wrote anything down, and all of their knowledge was passed on through oral tradition alone—in Socrates' case, his ideas were captured by Plato and Xenophon, and with Orunmila, his students committed important ideas to memory.

The comparison between these two thinkers is intriguing. Olúwolé believed that Socrates and Orunmila shared about 75 percent of the same philosophical views of the world, even though they had incredibly different geographic and cultural backgrounds.

Searching for the Truth

Socrates was aware of the limits of human knowledge and understanding. But most importantly, he was acutely conscious of his own ignorance. He would say that he knew that he knew nothing, which was unbelievably powerful.

> "TRUE WISDOM COMES TO EACH OF US WHEN WE REALIZE HOW LITTLE WE UNDERSTAND ABOUT LIFE, OURSELVES, AND THE WORLD AROUND US."
>
> SOCRATES

This made him incredibly open-minded. He believed that discussing topics and ideas was the most important way to make progress within them. Nothing was off-limits.

Being able to talk about any subject objectively and fairly is essential if we want to live in a free society. The biggest enemy of critical thinking is a lack of open debate around any subject. Everything should be on the table if we are to be able to think critically about it. It will be hard to find objective truth if we are limited by what we can and can't discuss.

A tactic often employed to undermine opposing narratives is silencing them—a strategy straight from the tyrant's handbook and relevant to countless ancient examples. The absence of debate shields viewpoints from challenge and is a method tyrants and dictators have used to maintain control. Socrates himself fell victim to this tactic; the powers that be hated him for asking so many questions and being openly critical of Athenian society. So, they made up an excuse to kill him.

In a world where the boundaries of truth are becoming blurred (thanks to AI and photo- and video-editing software), our quest for knowledge and truth is more important than ever.

When everything we see online can look incredibly convincing, thanks to this potential digital enhancement, we need to bring real discernment to the table to avoid being manipulated. To keep the spirit of Socrates alive, we mustn't be afraid to ask questions and think critically. This will help us navigate modern times like a world-class homing pigeon.

Embracing the art of critical thinking is wonderful for boosting your problem-solving skills, improving communication, sharpening decision-making, and keeping an open mind to exciting new ideas. Let critical thinking be your guide to alternative ways of seeing the world!

Seriously Happy Hack

If we become conscious of the fact that we don't know that much but balance this with a mind that curiously asks questions, we will connect to the core foundation of Socrates' philosophy.

The Challenges

Drum roll please ... The fabric of reality is ready to be shaken. The curtains are getting pulled back, and the lights are shining brightly. So, get ready to develop your critical thinking and strengthen your intellectual prowess:

1 Puzzle It Out

An awesome way to challenge your thinking and cultivate a mind that operates outside the box is with puzzles and games that can push your mind in many different directions. Take chess, for example. The potential for complexity in the game of chess is mind-boggling. The same goes for sudoku puzzles in the "difficult" category—you know, the ones that drive you to the gates of despair and back. Yeah, they're fun and will stretch your mind.

There are so many fascinating puzzles and games to try, but here are a few you could explore as a starter:

- chess
- sudoku
- crosswords (including cryptic!)
- video games
- brain training apps
- board games with friends (something that will encourage strategy is best).

2   Why, Oh Why?

Curiosity is a powerful force. We increase our understanding of reality by asking deeper questions about the world around us. Sometimes, things aren't as they seem and may require further investigation. Untangling this web is what Socrates was all about. So, in the spirit of asking questions, here are some topics for you to independently research and think about. Feel free to add to the list. Just start asking more questions. My suggestions below are interesting topics for you to ponder. Start pulling at these threads, and see what happens:

- What is fiat currency?
- What is simulation theory?
- How were the pyramids of Egypt built?
- Who created the modern education system?
- Who invented the Internet?
- What is the Fermi Paradox?
- Why is "casu marzu" the world's most dangerous cheese?
- What is decentralization?

3   A Difference Perspective

Read a book, listen to a podcast, or watch a documentary that will challenge your current perspective on the world. Looking at subjects from multiple angles allows us to think more critically about them.

The goal is to deliberately seek out opinions that greatly differ from yours and absorb yourself in them.

Try to understand things from a different perspective: "What do you mean you hate celery ... How could you?!" becomes: "You hate celery? Hmmm. Interesting. Tell me more."

Learn to pay attention to how it feels when your ideas are challenged head-on.

In a way, a great method of exploring this is to perform the Socratic Method on your own life—what beliefs do you currently hold that are contradictory? Where are you hypocritical? How could you change this to bring your thinking more into alignment?

Don't worry. Most of us are guilty of holding contradictory beliefs, but we aren't fully aware of them. Spending some time looking into different perspectives can help us see these inconsistencies. This whole process can be very transformative.

Chapter 4

A WORKOUT FOR YOUR WELL-BEING

Taoism

The alarm went off, but it was still dark. The unfamiliar surroundings confused me as I took a few seconds to remember where I was. But then, like a lightning strike, a pang of excitement filled my body. Something special was about to happen ...

I crawled out of my sleeping bag and quickly got dressed, making my way out of the tent and into the darkness. The air was crisp and cold, the sky inky black with an impressive spread of sparkling stars. The wide, empty Sahara Desert surrounded me in all directions. There was no light pollution, and everything felt incredibly still.

I headed away from our camp and toward the biggest sand dune I could (just about) make out. It was an easy climb to the top, but every step filled me with joy and excitement. At the crest of the dune, I sat down and looked around. And then waited. After some time, the sky began to change. The sunrise that followed completely blew my mind. The intense pink, red, orange, and yellow hues brought an ethereal quality to the desert. It was awe-inspiring. I will never forget that sunrise for the rest of my life. Getting there had taken a lot of effort, but the reward was worth it. The peace and tranquility I experienced in that moment were priceless.

Time in nature always makes me feel good, and I absolutely love seeking out new places.

Importantly, this time in nature doesn't need to be an epic trip to the Sahara; it can be found in my local surroundings, whether it's my backyard, a nearby park, or any green space that brings me solace. It's something that I highly value because it brings me a sense of calm and a deeper connection to the world. This has become an essential part of my well-being tool kit over the years.

Well-being is a broad term that refers to the overall state of feeling mentally and physically balanced. It's a holistic concept that encompasses all areas of life, from being healthy and happy to finding contentment and adopting a positive mindset.

It's important in life to be conscious of your well-being. Are you feeling OK? Balanced? Ready to go? Checking in with yourself is crucial. Right now:

◎ How are you?
◎ How's your mental health?
◎ Are you feeling in control of your mind?
◎ How's your physical health?
◎ Are you in pain anywhere?
◎ How's your body feeling today?

These types of questions bring awareness to your current state (both physical and mental). When you stop to check in, this allows you to connect with yourself, which is a wonderful thing. Unfortunately, this is something that a lot of us aren't used to and, therefore, are not that great at doing.

During my period of intense anxiety and panic attacks, my mental and physical well-being were at rock bottom. I was out of balance in many ways in my life. I hadn't been taking care of myself, and I'd certainly not been checking in with how I felt. You see, I was very unhealthy in many ways and had collected a series of bad habits: eating junk food, smoking, not sleeping properly, consuming negative content, playing zombie video games for hours on end, getting locked into unhelpful self-talk, and not exercising.

Reflecting on this tumultuous period, I realized that my panic attacks were not isolated incidents, but rather a gradual buildup of disharmony within me. This helped me truly understand the importance of well-being. As I began to recover, I started to appreciate the things that made me feel good. Healthy eating, exercising, sleeping well, reading philosophy books, and spending time in nature became a priority.

These days, when life gets overwhelming and I feel uneasy, I know that I need to carve out time to prioritize my well-being.

You might be feeling fantastic right now. But you might not. Either way, understanding how to optimize your well-being will greatly improve your life. The next group of philosophers we meet offers timeless guidance on navigating life's complexities and maintaining harmony and happiness amid the chaos. Trust me, you're going to love them.

Dip a Toe in the Tao

Taoism (pronounced "Daoism") is an ancient Chinese philosophy that encourages us to find balance in our lives by working with the natural world around us. There's a real focus on finding calmness, composure, and tranquillity through living well. The Taoists take a holistic approach to well-being and recommend spending time in nature, learning to relax, appreciating the arts, eating well, exercising, and meditating.

The philosophy evolved from early mystic and shamanistic practices in ancient China, where there was a deep understanding of nature. These ideas melded with influences from Indian Buddhism to eventually become what we now know as Taoism. Taoism began its journey around 500 BCE, or perhaps earlier, initially taking on a more philosophical tone. It later embraced religious aspects, even becoming a semiofficial religion of China at one point.

In modern times, you'll find Taoist practitioners all over the world. Most of them are located in China and Taiwan, but you'll also be able to find them in the West. It's hard to give exact numbers of Taoist practitioners, with estimates ranging from 12 million to a whopping 170 million—let's play it safe and settle for millions.

The pioneers of early philosophical Taoism include Lao-tzu, Chuang Tzu and Leih Tzu. These three are widely credited as being the driving forces behind its creation and development. Lao-tzu, often regarded as the most influential, is attributed with crafting the *Tao Te Ching* (pronounced "Dao De Jeng") around 500 BCE. It's a beautiful book that contains 81 chapters with concise wisdom on how to live well—and is the core text of the philosophy. The title can roughly be translated as "the way of integrity".

Legend has it that Lao-tzu, fed up with society, decided to leave China and head to the mountains beyond the Chinese border to become a hermit. He was a respected philosopher at the time and very popular. When he reached the border, the guard at the gate asked Lao-tzu to write down some important lessons before he left. In that instance, he created the *Tao Te Ching*—which just happened to become one of the most influential books of all time. That's the legend, anyway.

It is said that Lao-tzu went to spend the rest of his life living remotely in nature. He was never seen again, but his words have echoed throughout the ages and left an incredible impression on future generations.

Tao & Nature

Tao (pronounced "Dao") is, of course, a big concept in Taoism. It's so important that the whole philosophy is named after it ... But here's the tricky part: you can't really define it with words. In fact, the Taoists say that it defies definition. If we attempt to put it into words, we won't be able to convey it. The *Tao Te Ching* opens with these words from Lao-tzu, which make this exact point: "Tao called Tao is not Tao."

No names can capture it. However, we can have a try ...

Technically, Tao translates to "Way" or "Way of the Universe." A little confusing, right? We might be better off thinking about it like this:

Tao is the origin of everything.

It could be thought of as the universe itself and the fundamental laws of nature. You can almost think of it as a kind of force that we're all a part of (a little like the Force in *Star Wars*).

Tao is super-influenced by nature. Taoists spent a lot of time observing the natural world, and through that they developed their insight into how the universe operates. By recognizing patterns and cycles, they understood the interconnectedness of all things in life.

By spending time outside, we learn to have a deeper understanding of nature. The deeper our understanding, the more we care about the natural world. This connection is grounding and can help with our overall sense of well-being.

Close to where I live, a kingfisher comes to visit every winter. To my previous self (before getting deeper into Taoism), this would have simply been a random blue bird. I didn't know what it was called. I would just see lots of people getting very excited. Yeah, it was a cool bird, but how excited should I be about it? Anyway, when I started investigating bird facts and learning about kingfishers, I became more interested in them. I began to care. These sightings weren't that common, and I was lucky enough to witness them so regularly. There was something special about this bird.

Each time I saw it, I appreciated it even more. The electric blue and green on its back were stunning. There was something calming and peaceful about observing the kingfisher, and I grew really fond of seeing it.

The ancient Taoists knew how important our connection to nature was.

They would write, paint and create music based on the inspiration they found in the wild. They really understood how powerful it is to soak in the great outdoors.

I BELIEVE I CAN FLY

The Taoist method of observing nature and trying to understand it has led to some innovative designs and inventions in China. The acrobatic kite and the hang glider were developed by Taoists thousands of years ago in the Chinese mountains to help them understand the laws of nature. What better way to learn about the wind than to fly?

Wu Wei

A way of working with the Tao (Way of the Universe) is to develop a go-with-the-flow attitude. There's a phrase for this—"Wu Wei"—and it can roughly be translated as "actionless action." This idea is at the core of how the Taoists live and means to work with events rather than against them. It's a little like the bird that effortlessly rides the wind currents or water flowing smoothly around obstacles.

The beauty of living the Wu Wei way is that we start developing our intuition—our ability to understand or respond instinctively to something. This is a subtle art that is often neglected in Western culture. When we develop this intuition, we get better at checking in with ourselves. We understand who we are more deeply. Intuition is integral to our well-being, and learning to listen to our gut and heart can help provide us with an often untapped source of wisdom.

From a Western perspective, we are very much encouraged to think with our heads, and in fact a great deal of the philosophical groundwork that underpins Western society is based on this. Just look at most of the Western philosophies in this book ... Reasoning and logic are often front and center. This is all well and good, but we would be prudent to balance this type of thinking with our intuition.

There are countless incredible stories about people following their intuition and experiencing some unbelievable events on the back of this. A friend of mine has a remarkable story about losing her son in a busy Moroccan market while on vacation in Marrakech. After being somewhat distracted by the hustle and bustle of the souk stalls, she turned around to discover that her little boy had suddenly disappeared! Not stopping to think or freak out, she followed her gut and just headed through the intricate maze of narrow lanes straight to where her son had wandered off to. My friend told me that she knew where he was but couldn't explain how she knew it. Her intuition had taken over. Ask around, and see what stories your friends and family members have based on following their intuition.

Qi

One of the key ways that Taoists cultivate their well-being is through the ancient arts of Tai Chi and Qigong. You may have seen people practicing Tai Chi—it looks like a wonderful slow-motion fight with an invisible opponent. And then there's Qigong, where someone might mimic the postures and movements of animals.

Technically, Tai Chi is a traditional Chinese martial art heavily influenced by Taoist philosophy. It can be practiced in a group, in one-on-one combat (without full contact), or solo. There are many schools of Tai Chi and countless forms to learn. The forms are a series of repeated movements, but one single form of Tai Chi can take months to learn and a lifetime to master. Qigong, on the other hand, is often one single move repeated over and over. Sometimes, it doesn't involve movement at all and will focus on breathing.

Both practices are performed slowly and smoothly in a meditative manner to cultivate energy and improve health. At times, they might look like a graceful dance to the onlooker. Unless you're watching me do it, then it's more like watching a badger navigate its way through an overgrown hedge—but I'm working on it!

Honestly, these practices are way more challenging than they might initially look. I have learned Tai Chi and Qigong forms over the years, and they require a lot of coordination but are excellent ways of exercising both the body and mind, helping them to synchronize.

According to the Taoists (and many other Chinese philosophies), there's this thing called chi or qi, which is like our vital energy or life force. Taoists created Tai Chi and Qigong to help establish and maintain the balance of chi within the body.

When this energy is balanced, it is believed to bring about good mental, physical, and spiritual health.

Imagine it like a healthy, smooth-flowing river—when it's not blocked, we will find harmony in our lives.

It's worth noting that many ancient cultures reference the same kind of vital energy. In India, it's called prana. In Japan, it's ki. In Polynesia, mana, and in some Native American cultures, it's known as the Great Spirit. Taking care of our vital energy to help keep us feeling balanced and healthy is, therefore, a universal idea.

Needles & Herbs

Bao Gu was a legendary Chinese female Taoist doctor from the fourth Century. She became well-known for her mastery of acupuncture and herbal remedies—two modalities commonly associated with Taoism. They predominately focus on rebalancing qi within the body to help the patient restore harmony. Acupuncture does this by inserting fine needles into different pressure points around the body, and herbal remedies are taken by ingesting or applying a specific combination of plants, roots and herbs. These ancient practices have been around for thousands of years and are still incredibly popular in the modern world.

The story of Bao Gu is fascinating. There are tales about her curing patients with unusual diseases, healing whole villages with her plant knowledge, and becoming such a master of alchemy that she supposedly became immortal. This is where myth and legend meet. I'm not saying she's still alive in the Chinese mountains—or is she?

Taoism is calm and beautiful and can be fantastic for developing our well-being. There's so much more to discover about the philosophy, and I hope that you get the chance to explore it further.

Seriously Happy Hack

The Taoists encourage us to cultivate well-being with a well-rounded approach to life. If we learn to go with the flow, follow our intuition, connect with nature, relax, and practice art forms like Tai Chi and Qigong, we will balance both body and mind.

The Challenges

Try these Taoist-inspired challenges to help cultivate your well-being.

1 Tai Chi & Qigong

For this challenge, the goal is to learn a simple Tai Chi and Qigong form. This is essentially a short sequence of choreographed movements.

Learning a basic Tai Chi form is a wonderful way to connect with Taoism. Something like the **Tai Chi Eight Form** is a good place to start. There are thousands of online videos and instructions to get you started.

If you want to take it further, you could try learning a simple **Tai Chi Sword Form**. This is Tai Chi but with a sword. Thankfully, you don't have to use an actual sword—a pole, stick, cardboard tube, baguette, or light saber would do the trick just as well. If your neighbor questions why you're in the yard wielding a baguette, just tell them about Tai Chi and Taoism and how powerful they are for your well-being—and they might join you!

Qigong is another wonderful way to lean into Taoist philosophy. A lot of Qigong forms follow nature and natural laws. One of the most famous forms is **Five Animal Qigong**. This is based on a series of movements inspired by a Tiger, Deer, Bear, Monkey, and Crane. It's a relatively simple routine but has many variations. Start by learning this form—a quick search online will give you plenty of options.

As with Tai Chi, Qigong has many different schools and forms to explore. Whichever school you choose, you'll still be pretending that you're a bear in your living room ... which is actually a lot more fun than you might think.

Both of these Taoist practices can be a calming, grounding, and peaceful way to start the day. So, why not try them out when you first wake up and begin the day with the serenity and composure of a Taoist?

2   The Great Outdoors

The Taoists have a deep respect for the natural world and believe that spending time immersed in the outdoors is essential for optimizing well-being.

For this challenge, you need to carve out some time to sit quietly and observe nature. This will depend on where you live and what natural environments you might have nearby. It can be done in a park, forest, on a hill, beach, in the mountains, or by a pond or lake.

As you sit there, try and look closely at the environment around you.

◎ What patterns can you see in nature?
◎ What impact does the current season have on what you are looking at?
◎ What animals or other creatures are you aware of?

Learning more about the natural world is a great way of connecting to it on a deeper level. This connection can be a profound experience as you uncover layers of beauty and complexity in things that often get taken for granted. The patterns in tree bark, widening ripples on water, and the influence of the sun on the shape of trees are just a few examples. Being able to spot these layers of beauty and complexity is incredibly inspiring.

If I feel a little stressed, a good walk in the park and some time spent outdoors in the fresh air makes me feel so much better. I love being by water and find it incredibly calming. If I can squeeze in an open-air swim somewhere, even better. These activities are food for my soul.

3   Wu Wei Adventure

As we explored earlier, Wu Wei roughly means "go with the flow." So, go somewhere that you've never been before; be guided by your curiosity, go with the flow, and see what happens ...

I'm not talking about climbing unnamed mountains in remote parts of the world here. I'm just suggesting going somewhere new and unfamiliar (avoiding danger or getting lost, of course). Decide on a location and spend some time exploring it. Try not to use your phone or look at maps to plan routes. Instead, try and tap into your intuition on your Wu Wei adventure.

This challenge is amazing for developing your gut feeling, which in turn helps you to be better connected with yourself—an essential part of cultivating well-being.

When I was 18, a group of us traveled by train around Europe for several months and ended up living the Wu Wei way. The trip was completely spontaneous; we didn't book hotels or hostels beforehand. We planned almost nothing, so each day, we would head out on an adventure and go with the flow. For the most part, things worked out.

Of course, it wasn't always perfect, and there were several times when things got tricky, but this always led to another adventure and a story to tell on the back of it. Not knowing what the next stop in your trip is can be both frightening and liberating.

I learned so much from that experience, namely that there is something very empowering about going with the flow.

Chapter 5:
SUPERCHARGE YOUR MINDSET

I've failed at things countless times ... I've crashed bikes, fallen off climbs, and been chased by angry cows. I've gotten terrible results on tests, been rejected multiple times, oh, and lost stuff. I've messed up important meetings, broken things by accident, and broken things on purpose—I confess, not some of my finest moments. I've worked terrible jobs, slipped, tripped, and tumbled over objects, and said the wrong thing at the worst possible time. Once, I even accidentally ran into the pond in my good friend's yard, fully clothed. It was dark, OK?

We all make mistakes or fail at some point in our lives. Stuff going wrong and plans falling apart is inevitable.

Yes, it sucks, but learning to work with this universal law is a lot better than trying to fight it kicking and screaming. The goal is to turn this force into a positive thing. I know failure doesn't seem like it could ever be a positive thing. But it can be—trust me. If we learn how to frame it correctly, we can take advantage of the lessons that failure teaches us.

One of my most intense experiences of facing failure was during an alpine climb in the European Alps. My friend Matt and I had a big list of 13,000-foot mountains that we were planning to climb. Unfortunately, the weather forecast was useless for our climbing window. Instead of accepting this, we decided to cram in as much as possible in two days before a massive storm rolled in. Yes, you can probably guess where this is going ... The thing with high-altitude climbing is that you need to acclimatize properly over several days. If you climb without letting your body adjust, you are going to suffer. And that can be dangerous.

Well, like a pair of stubborn idiots, we plowed through the altitude sickness, thinking that our fitness would see us through. After two days of intense hiking and climbing, we found ourselves in a hut on top of Monte Rosa—a 14,760-foot icy mountain in Italy. But we were suffering from our lack of acclimatizing; my body just couldn't warm up. It was very frightening. To make matters worse, we witnessed someone getting airlifted off the mountain because of altitude sickness. The helicopter swooped in to rescue this person, and we wanted to jump on board but couldn't. The fact that someone else was so ill from the altitude was frightening. What was the next stage of altitude sickness? Would our conditions deteriorate further? What did we need to do? Our inexperience and lack of planning came at a price.

Thankfully, we made a good decision at that point and forced ourselves to descend as quickly as possible and abandon all our plans for the rest of the climb. It was an exhausting descent, but with every step, we started to feel our souls return to our bodies. Many lessons were learned that day—mainly about knowing when to quit and understanding our personal tolerance for risk. The fact that the climb was a "failure" didn't matter. We were happy we got through that situation and learned something about ourselves along the way.

The reality is that we will all have challenging experiences in life. Some of these will be self-induced (like our crazy mountain climbing experience) or the result of choosing to do something

77

difficult. Other times, we will have tough experiences in life that we definitely didn't sign up for. Sometimes, life is hard, and we can get hurt. Sometimes, we face setbacks and challenges that push us to our limits. How we deal with these instances is everything ... What matters is our mindset.

Growth vs. Fixed Mindset

Imagine your mindset as the lens through which you see and approach life. In modern psychology, there are two different types of mindsets, and they can have a big impact on how you handle challenges and view yourself. They are called a growth mindset and a fixed mindset.

A fixed mindset is like thinking, "I am how I am, and that's that." If you have a fixed mindset, you might believe that if you mess something up, that's a sign that you shouldn't do it. You might believe that if you struggle, it means you're not naturally good at something. This can make you avoid trying new things and make it tough to take risks. It's a very closed-minded outlook on life.

A growth mindset is like having a can-do attitude. You believe that your abilities and intelligence can improve and grow. Challenges and difficult experiences are seen as opportunities to learn. When things get tough, you don't give up. Instead, you see it as a chance to develop new skills and look for solutions to your problems.

While setbacks and mistakes are inevitable, a persistent and positive approach to life's challenges can significantly boost your happiness.

So, as the saying goes: when life gives you lemons, make lemonade. Or my favorite: when life gives you avocados, make guacamole. Either way, you're making something out of what you've got. This attitude aligns with the philosophy of Stoicism, which emphasizes embracing life's challenges and making the most of every situation. Developing a growth mindset is central to the philosophy of Stoicism, and it allows us to navigate life's twists and turns with wisdom and resilience.

Stoicism

Stoicism seriously saved me and transformed my mind in a profoundly positive way. When I was in that dark pit of anxiety, Stoic ideas were the rope that helped me climb out. They also acted as a gateway to other philosophies and inspired me to get deeper into the whole subject, which has made my life so much happier in many ways. It's safe to say that I owe the Stoics a lot.

There are so many wonderfully pragmatic ideas from this ancient Greek and Roman philosophy that can help us in countless ways. There's a real emphasis on:

- developing a virtuous character
- learning how to handle the ups and downs of life
- tips for mastering the mind
- ideas for increasing gratitude
- advice on dealing with powerful emotions.

We are spoiled for choice.

The primary aim of Stoicism is to achieve eudaemonia, which refers to a fulfilling state of life and a holistic approach to happiness, as we discussed on page 4.

Eudaemonia goes beyond momentary pleasure and emphasizes a deeper sense of well-being, purpose, and flourishing in one's overall existence.

According to Stoic philosophy, there are many ways to achieve this but the fundamental belief is that by developing a virtuous character, we will be well on our way to achieving this elusive eudaemonia.

From Shipwrecks to Emperors

Interestingly, Stoicism was forged after a pretty epic setback. Around 300 BCE, a man from Cyprus named Zeno established the philosophy after an unfortunate event. He was sailing his goods across the Mediterranean when he suffered a shipwreck and lost everything in an instant. The accident wiped out his business selling purple dye (extracted from sea snails and used to dye the royal robes of kings and queens). It was a disaster. Luckily, he survived.

Following this, Zeno found himself in Athens and became interested in philosophy, supposedly as a way to work through the mental torment of losing all of his wealth overnight. He began studying with a Cynic philosopher named Crates of Thebes. Zeno undertook a whole program of philosophy training in which Crates encouraged Zeno to deliberately seek out discomfort.

After studying for a while, Zeno felt confident enough to establish his own school ... and Stoicism was born. He then began lecturing at the Stoa Poikile—a giant painted porch in the Agora, Athens. This is where the word "Stoicism" comes from, since the name is based on the geographic location where the philosophy was established, not the founder.

Over time, the philosophy grew in popularity. Various heads of the school developed the tradition over the years and put their own stamp on it. Stoicism spread throughout ancient Greece and eventually made its way to Rome. It gained notoriety when the Roman Emperor, Marcus Aurelius, became an avid follower. He is arguably Stoicism's most famous proponent and helped to propel Stoicism to a wider audience and greater popularity.

The Roman period was a prolific time for the Stoics, and thankfully, we still have a lot of writings from this era. The Stoic philosopher Seneca contributed a large body of work here, Marcus Aurelius left us his book *Meditations*, and Musonius Rufus gave us some wonderful snippets of Stoic wisdom such as:

"YOU WILL DESERVE RESPECT FROM EVERYONE IF YOU WILL START BY RESPECTING YOURSELF."

MUSONIUS RUFUS

There's some excellent wisdom to explore from these Roman philosophers. Unfortunately, most books and articles from the Greek period have been lost or destroyed due to complacency or malice. Nowadays, Stoicism has had a resurgence of interest—books are being published and people are talking about Stoic philosophy online. Stoicism became popularized by various writers, entrepreneurs, athletes, world leaders, and musicians—from George Washington to Toussaint Louverture to Tom Hiddleston. It has even influenced modern mental health therapies—CBT (Cognitive Behavioral Therapy), and REBT (Rational Emotive Behavior Therapy)—the founders of these practices being big fans of the Stoics.

THE WORLD'S FUNNIEST JOKE

The third head of the Stoic school was a man named Chrysippus. He helped to spread Stoicism by lecturing outside of the Stoa Poikile. He was the first person to hit up the big venues outside of the Agora of Athens—almost like he was on some sort of Stoic world tour. Yep, Chrysippus was kind of a rock star.

Anyway, there's a strange legend surrounding his death. One day, Chrysippus cracked a joke that was so funny that he died from laughing too much. Apparently, his gag was so sidesplittingly hilarious that he just couldn't stop laughing, until he eventually keeled over with exhaustion and left this world. He died laughing (at his own joke). What a way to go.

The Stoics believed that it's not what happens to us in life that matters but how we respond to it.

Things will inevitably go wrong, and we will make mistakes, but we can choose where we go and how we respond from that point. We decide what to do next. This is a growth mindset in action. We might not be able to stop the rain, but we can take an umbrella. Dropped your dinner on the floor? No problem. The floor is now your table. (OK, not sure about that one, but you get my point ...)

The Stoics felt that we *always* have a choice about how we respond in life. The legendary Greek Stoic philosopher Epictetus held this as his mantra. Epictetus' life was incredibly challenging since he was born into slavery and suffered a severe leg injury that meant he had to walk with a stick.

After gaining his freedom from slavery, he went on to set up a school of Stoic philosophy, where he promoted the idea that we are free to choose our response to external events. This was his way of handling the hardships and setbacks he encountered throughout his life. His influence on philosophy has been huge, and his writing remains a core part of the teachings.

He truly exemplified a Stoic life.

Epictetus taught his students to handle whatever came their way with calm composure and equanimity. He suggested a very practical way of doing this—by focusing on what you CAN actually control in any given situation.

Imagine you're getting ready for a virtual gaming tournament, and suddenly your Internet crashes right before a crucial match. It's a total nightmare, but there's no time to get frustrated. Following Epictetus' advice would mean shifting your focus to what you *can* control in this situation. Instead of dwelling on the technical glitch, think about what immediate actions you can take—maybe troubleshooting your Internet connection, contacting the organizers for a brief delay, or seeing if you can saucily ask your neighbor to connect to their Wi-Fi. It's about staying calm under pressure and finding practical solutions to the issues you can influence in the moment. That's the kind of approach Epictetus would applaud.

Learning to understand what we can and can't control in any given situation is officially called "The Dichotomy of Control." However, I like to call it Stoicism's Golden Rule. This is mainly because it highlights how integral it is to the core of the philosophy, but also because it just sounds cooler.

The connection to a growth mindset becomes clear when we look for insights from our experiences in hindsight.

The Stoics were big advocates of journaling, using it as a tool for daily reflection.

In fact, Epictetus' teachings encourage us to reflect on what went well, what went badly, and what's left to be done as a daily practice. It's a simple task but one that can help us learn from each experience we encounter. Looking back through the setbacks and failures of the day can be empowering if we look for lessons. This way, we are giving value to the difficult experiences we face.

It's a great way of reframing problems. This is a "growing through what you go through" attitude.

> "IT'S NOT WHAT HAPPENS TO YOU, BUT HOW YOU REACT TO IT THAT MATTERS."
>
> EPICTETUS

The Stoic Opposition

Accepting what can and can't be controlled doesn't mean that the Stoics were passive or resigned. It's not about saying, "Oh, let's give up and have a snack." It's more about understanding where to direct our attention. You see, Stoicism's Golden Rule can be used in many settings, including navigating challenging political environments filled with obstacles and setbacks. Read on …

During the Roman Emperor Nero's reign (from 54 CE to 68 CE), a collective of Stoics started to push back against his tyranny, mainly through political activity. They became referred to as the Stoic Opposition. Nero was deeply resented by a lot of people because he wielded his power in a very disturbing way. He had his own mother killed, manipulated the legal system to eliminate rivals and dissenters, and engaged in extravagant and wasteful spending, which contributed to economic hardship for the Roman population. The Stoic Opposition, which included key figures like Thrasea, became a target of Nero's wrath. In response to the perceived threat, Nero had Thrasea executed and exiled many other members of the Stoic Opposition.

The Stoic practitioner Fannia (d. 103 CE) stood out as a political rebel within this collective, enduring multiple exiles to unfavorable locations due to her association with the Stoic Opposition. When her Stoic husband was exiled, she followed him. He was later executed for his involvement with this group, and Fannia faced yet another exile later in life for being involved with a book that praised her husband and his work with the collective. Unfazed by court interrogations from Nero's governance, she openly shared details without worrying about the consequences—it was her idea to create the book, although allegedly she did not write it. Fannia wasn't intimidated by Nero's tyranny and didn't even try to disguise her connection to the Opposition group. Thanks to this, she was banished to faraway lands but managed to save her husband's diaries and biography in the process.

Fannia had a reputation as respectable and mentally strong, and she was said to live a life of virtue. She exhibited a growth mindset to whatever obstacles she faced and kept moving forward despite setbacks.

Although it might have been difficult to fight back against tyranny, the Stoic Opposition did all they could. By focusing on what could actually be done and staying strong when things didn't go to plan, they gained an excellent reputation and inspired countless others. We can learn a lot from these philosophers that can be applied to our lives today.

Seriously Happy Hack

The Stoics believe that how you respond to life events is critical. When facing a setback, challenge, or failure, focus on what you can actually control in that situation. Put your attention here. And try not to worry about the things outside of your control. Learn from your mistakes, and keep a growth mindset in your approach.

The Challenges

The Stoics chased the state of eudaemonia. For them, a mind that is able to handle the challenges that inevitably come our way is a happy mind. When we get good at handling setbacks and failure, it can help us to feel more prepared for life. So, in the spirit of Stoicism, why not summon your inner Zeno, Epictetus, and Fannia by trying some of these challenges.

1 The Control List

OK, crisis management, Stoic-style. When you're dealing with a big problem (or even a small crisis, as in the example below), use this template to keep in control of the situation.

1. Write down your problem, challenge, or setback.
Example—*I've planned a party for my best friend, and the venue has canceled at the last minute.*

2. Write down all of the things that you CAN'T control.
- *I don't have a lot of time to solve the problem.*
- *I can't control how the guests will respond if I have to cancel the entire party.*
- *I can't control how my best friend will feel.*

3. Write down all of the things that you CAN control.
- *I can try hard to find another venue at the last minute.*
- *I can ask people for help.*
- *I can keep everyone updated on last-minute changes.*
- *I can figure out how to deliver the news to my best friend if I can't find a new venue in time.*

4. Put ALL of your focus on the "things you can control" list.
- Keep your attention here, and build solutions to the problem, setback, or failure.

5. Don't stress about the "things you can't control" list.
- You can put this one to the side or even leave it in a corner somewhere.

I've used this method when facing many setbacks in my life and can now reel off a "can or can't control list" in my head quite quickly. If it's a particularly thorny problem, writing a physical list in a notebook is best. I know this all sounds like common sense—and that's because it is. However, it's amazing how easy it is to forget a simple but helpful process like this in a crisis.

2   Write a "Setback Diary"

"Dear Diary, today sucked ..."

Journaling or writing in a diary is a great way to develop a growth mindset. The Roman Stoic Seneca journaled in the morning and the evening. Marcus Aurelius' *Meditations*, which was essentially his journal, became one of the most important philosophy books on the planet. Many modern Stoics encourage this practice, too.

Creating a setback diary is a powerful tool that can help us gain value from setbacks and failures. At the end of each day, write down all the problems you encountered. Big or small, it doesn't matter. Even things that feel minor, such as: "My new toothbrush package was difficult to open" or "Tripped on a curb" can make it to the journal. Fill the page with as many setbacks as you can for each day.

You then need to rank yourself out of ten for how you handled said setback (1—Awful / 10—Amazing). If you handled it smoothly, give yourself a 10. If you had a meltdown, maybe a one would be more fitting.

Analyzing your response to challenges will help you to get better at dealing with them in the future. First, bring awareness. Then, you can alter your behavior. The goal is, of course, to aim for all 10s—but I'd say that is pretty much impossible—so go easy on yourself, and build up to them!

3 Collector of Random Skills

The goal of this challenge is to push the mind by learning new skills —the more challenging, the better. This is where you may well encounter elements of failure and frustration, because when you learn something new, failure and setbacks will be an inevitable part of the learning experience. Working with this can be powerful and help you to build a resilient mind capable of handling setbacks.

Some skills you could learn:

- juggling
- origami
- knitting or crochet
- a new language
- an instrument
- cooking something technical like a soufflé
- solve a Rubik's cube
- a magic trick.

Pick a couple of skills to get started.

Pay attention to your mindset when you make mistakes—the aim is to try and get comfortable with the process of failing along the way.

Chapter 6:
DECISION TIME:
CHOOSE AWESOME

My decision to move from the countryside to the city felt like a phenomenally difficult one. It was a leap into the unknown, and with that came a certain amount of pressure. I knew that I wanted to do it, but it felt intimidating. I kept second-guessing myself. Was this the right thing for me to do? Should I *really* move to London? Will I be OK on my own? Self-doubts occupied my mind.

I'd deferred my place at college for a year so that I could travel, which ended up being one of the best decisions of my life. But when the time had finally come for me to move to the city, I felt hesitant. I wanted to study music, and since my college was right in the heart of London, I had to leave my familiar countryside surroundings. There were opportunities in the city, but moving away from home for the first time seemed overwhelming. It felt tough having to make such a big life decision. Having a "roadmap" for making this decision that would allow me to feel confident with my choice would have been helpful, but it was years before I found a roadmap that would actually help me.

In the end, I grew so much from moving to the city. I loved my time in London and studying music led to some amazing adventures and experiences. The funny thing is, when I eventually decided to leave London, after well over a decade, I felt the same level of insecurity about my next move. The decision-making doubt had returned. It turns out it's not an age thing, it's a human thing!

After I discovered philosophy, my decision-making muscle got significantly stronger. My personal mantra these days is that there are no wrong decisions—only lessons and slightly different outcomes. The reality is that we're not always going to make the right decisions, but as long as we've learned something from the experience, we haven't really lost—we've just gained a deeper understanding of what we do or don't want. It took a long time for me to think this way, but it definitely feels like an empowering way to view decisions.

Over the years, I've had to make a lot of decisions. Some have been fun, such as which mountain to climb next. Some have been in scary situations, like when I'm lost in a whiteout on the mountainside: Which way do I go? Some have been around where to live, and some have been around work—is this the right job for me? Others have been completely life-defining, like getting married, having a kid, and writing books. All of these have made me who I am today.

It's not always easy to make decisions in life, and it can be tough figuring out which path to take when there are so many options.

And these options have implications ... If we're not careful, a series of bad decisions in a row could lead to dire consequences, but equally, a series of good decisions can transform our lives!

Thankfully, there are things we can do to help us choose the best way forward. In fact, there's a fantastic strategy you can apply to every decision you'll ever need to make. This concept comes from the ancient philosopher Aristotle. Aristotle's strategy for decision-making has been profoundly helpful in my life, and I know it can help you, too. But first, let's have a look at what Aristotle was all about ...

Aristotle (384–322 BCE) was one of the most important thinkers of all time. He led a remarkably productive life, contributing to a wide number of subjects, including philosophy, ethics, politics, biology, physics, metaphysics, logic, and poetry. Aristotle had many notable achievements. He was:

- The **Father of Logic**: Aristotle is frequently credited for his pioneering work in developing logical systems and principles.

- The **creator of the Scientific Method**: He played a pivotal role in shaping the scientific method, laying down the fundamentals for systematic inquiry and observation.

- Known for his **"Virtue Ethics"**: These form the basis for a large portion of Western morality, encouraging the development of moral character and virtues.

- Accomplished in **Zoology**: Aristotle helped establish this field of research by collecting very detailed accounts of many species.

- Influential in **Political Theory**: His political theories, presented in his famous works such as *Politics*, remain key and influential texts today.

Aristotle was born into a wealthy family. Both of his parents were doctors and passed on their love of academia to him. His inherited talents, coupled with the resources and support provided by his family, helped him to thrive intellectually. As he grew older, he

began studying with the famous Greek philosopher Plato at the Academy and excelled there. The Academy, founded by Plato in 387 BCE, was one of the first schools of philosophical and scientific learning in the Western world.

When Aristotle was at the height of his influence, he opened his own philosophy school called the Lyceum in 335 BCE. This move was partly because Plato failed to appoint him as head of the Academy. Aristotle was angry at being overlooked for the role, so he set up a rival school. He bought an old gymnasium and upgraded it by incorporating an enormous library. His decision to open the Lyceum marked a philosophical shift away from Plato, as Aristotle began to develop his own unique perspectives and teachings in this new school, such as studying the real world through observation.

Lectures at the Lyceum were open to the public and free to attend (again, this was likely because cash flow was not an issue for Aristotle). His followers and students became known as peripatetics because they used to walk and discuss philosophy in the cloisters of the building. The word for "walk" in Greek is "peripatos;" thus the name "peripatetics" was born for these strolling philosophers. Aristotle loved to ponder on philosophical ideas while walking—and I agree— you can't beat a good pondering session or conversation on the go.

While he was out walking, you could spot Aristotle from a mile off. He was known for his flashy style—he was particular about his wardrobe and loved wearing lots of rings.

Aristotle taught many students at his philosophy school. However, one of his most famous was a young Alexander the Great. He worked with the teenage Alexander for three years, yet it was pretty much a pointless endeavor. Though Aristotle wanted to teach Alexander good values and morals, Alexander learned nothing from Aristotle and proceeded to become a monster.

In Aristotle's later life, the consequences of his association with Alexander came back to haunt him. Following Alcxander's death in 323 BCE, the public turned against Aristotle. They hated what Alexander had done during his conquering rule, and now that he was out of the picture, they wanted to punish anyone who had ties with him. Since Aristotle had taught Alexander, he ended up on the hit list. Fearing the same fate as the famous philosopher Socrates, who had faced a death sentence, Aristotle chose to leave Athens to avoid potential harm. He spent the remainder of his days living outside the city, opting for a safer location away from the brewing hatred of the public.

NOT SO PERFECT

Aristotle may be one of the most famous philosophers of all time, but a few things have tarnished his reputation ... Firstly, his inability to curb Alexander the Great's ruthless behavior raised questions about the effectiveness of his teachings. Secondly, Aristotle's views on women reflected the attitudes of the time and have been criticized for being dismissive and unequal. Thirdly, he thought that certain individuals were naturally suited to be enslaved, which also reflected the social norms of his era. Fourthly, his belief that some physical traits would indicate a person's level of intelligence is considered discriminatory.

Scholars defend Aristotle by saying that he was happy to update his worldview and would be unlikely to hold these opinions in the modern world. They claim that these attitudes are more a reflection of the time in ancient Athens. However, it's worth recognizing that certain aspects of his beliefs and actions still clash with today's ethical standards. Either way, if you end up reading Aristotle, you'll likely notice these opinions, so I think it's something to be aware of. History isn't always pretty.

The Philosophy for Good Living

Aristotle believed that the meaning of life is to live up to our potential. In ancient Greek, this is known as "dynamis" and is about striving to achieve the best version of yourself.

It's not about what others are up to—it's about YOU and YOUR potential.

Aristotle believed that by living up to our potential, we are well on the way to living a happy life.

For Aristotle, eudaemonia was also an important part of his happiness equation (as it was for a lot of ancient Greek thinkers). Developing a life that flowed well and a mind that could handle the ups and downs was integral to his work. This led him to lean into the virtues, or qualities of character, that we should develop if we want to achieve eudaemonia. This is where his "virtue ethics" were born. These are built around a series of virtues like wisdom, courage, justice, and self-control. If you want to know more, check out his book *Nicomachean Ethics*, since this is the go-to read for a detailed analysis of his virtue ethics.

If we can learn to use the right amount of these virtues in various situations, we will find a good balance in life. For example, too much courage becomes foolhardy, and too little courage becomes cowardly. The goal is to hit the middle ground with these virtues.

Trying to climb a mountain that is too dangerous for my current climbing skill would be reckless and potentially dangerous. However, if I never pushed myself and was too scared to ever climb anything, that would hold me back. It's about finding the right amount of courage for me to fulfill my potential.

This whole concept has become known as Aristotle's Golden Mean and is a term you'll hear frequently in the world of philosophy. The ability to find the middle ground is also helpful when it comes to making decisions. This type of thinking brings balance to our behavior and, in turn, discourages us from being overly impulsive and irrational when making important life choices. Balance is the key.

How to Make a Decision

The best thing I've learned from Aristotle is his solid-gold advice for making decisions. The method is easy to follow, comprehensive, and versatile. Whatever decision you need to make, trust me, Aristotle has your back.

There are eight steps to this process. If you ponder each step, you will have considered your decision holistically and hopefully should have clarity on what to do. With a little practice, you'll be able to employ this method relatively quickly in your head without too much trouble. So, let's give it a try:

1. Don't rush

Whatever you do, don't make a decision in haste. Give yourself time to reflect and think things through. The first thing you must create is the space to think.

2. Look at ALL the facts

Spend time evaluating all the facts available around your decision. Do some detailed research, and build a picture of the key take-homes. Separate speculation from the truth, and get clear on what's what. You don't need to create a load of spreadsheets and pie charts (but if that's your way of working, go you!). Just bring everything together in one place, and spend some time pondering the facts.

3. Consult experts

This step is pretty self-explanatory—seek out relevant experts and their advice. Yes, I know experts can get things wrong, too.

And, yes, perhaps we shouldn't have blind faith, but it does make sense to consult someone who knows more than us about a subject, right?

4. Who is affected?

Think about how your decision will impact other people. Is your second cousin going to be bothered about you opening a cheese store? How about your buddy who is allergic to cheese? OK, you might not have to cast the net this wide, but considering how your decision impacts others is important.

5. Think about past experiences

This one is easy—think about stuff from the past. Have you personally experienced anything that relates to your decision? If so, what can that teach you? More generally, you can expand this to look at how similar decisions have played out historically.

6. What's the likely outcome?

Calculate the probability of specific outcomes. Yes, it's hard to be completely accurate here, but what DO you think will happen? Be realistic.

7. Consider the impact of luck (good and bad)

Think about how luck might impact your decision. What would good luck look like in this scenario? What about bad luck? Try and think about what unexpected things might happen. Expect the unexpected, and you won't be so surprised. I'm sorry your croissant business failed—I guess I didn't have governments banning the consumption of pastries on my bingo card for this year. But there we go ...

8. Be clearheaded when deciding

Don't make a decision when in a bad mental state. If you're tired, angry, giddy with excitement, scared, overrun with grief, or in serious physical pain, trying to make an important life decision will be more difficult than normal. It'll be hard to think clearly and easy to be swayed by the emotions you're feeling. So, wait until mental clarity has returned before making any significant choices.

As you can see, this method is fantastic for mulling over big and important decisions. Should I go to college? Should I take this job? Should I move to the coast? But it's not so convenient if you're in a coffee shop working through a list of drink choices ...

With a little practice, you can quickly become a fast-thinking, decisive hotshot by employing Aristotle's decision-making method in your head without too much trouble.

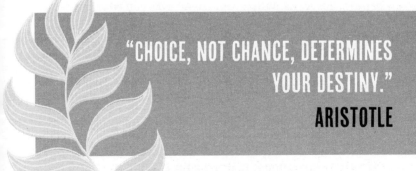

"CHOICE, NOT CHANCE, DETERMINES YOUR DESTINY."
ARISTOTLE

The Challenges

OK, it's time to become a more decisive human. Prepare the trumpets and confetti, and channel your inner Aristotle. Here are some ideas to help you make solid choices in life. The big ancient guy would be proud.

1 Decisions, Decisions!

A brilliantly simple way to become more decisive in life is ... to make more decisions. When your friend asks you what you want to watch, rather than say "I don't care," make a decision. Sure, you might not end up watching that movie or show, but the process of MAKING the decision is good practice—and this is the whole point of the task. The same goes for deciding what you want to eat, where you want to go with friends, or what you want to do. Give yourself permission to make decisions, and see it as an opportunity to try out your decision-making skills. Just like a real muscle, if you exercise it, it will grow bigger and stronger. However, if you need to make a more important decision, taking the time to work through Aristotle's method in detail will be worth it. Think about a particularly big decision that you have to make, and write down each step of his method. Then jot down how it applies to your situation.

Here's a quick reminder of the eight steps:

1. Don't rush.
2. Look at ALL the facts.
3. Consult experts.
4. Who is affected?
5. Think about past experiences.
6. What's the likely outcome?
7. Consider the impact of luck (good and bad).
8. Be clearheaded when deciding.

Learning to compress Aristotle's eight-step method into a quick mental model for decision-making is great for using on a daily basis. Every time you need to make a decision, whiz through the steps, and use them to guide you.

With practice, you'll become a decision-making pro.

2 Who Are You?

Aristotle particularly valued the virtue of self-knowledge. He considered this important for personal development and the quest for good character, which ties in nicely with making decisions. Learning more about yourself is a powerful way of making better choices in life.

When you are confident in who you are, making decisions that are right for you gets easier.

So, start looking a little deeper into what makes you tick. If you're incredibly creative but inhabit a very dry or uninspiring environment, you might feel an internal clash. All of this can be preemptively avoided if you make decisions that work well for you in the first place.

A great way to connect with yourself is by dipping into psychology. There are countless personality tests that you can have fun with, a personal favorite being the Myers-Briggs Type Indicator. This tool, widely used in psychology, assesses individuals across various personality dimensions, assigning them a four-letter type based on how they perceive and interact with the world. I found it accurate and insightful, but having said that, it's always best to take these tests with a pinch of salt. Don't get too hung up on what they say and get boxed in by your "type." Everyone is on a sliding scale, and most people will change as they progress through life. See it as a little fun but with the potential to learn about yourself in the process.

So, for this challenge, do some soul-searching and figure out more about who you are. You might also choose to ask friends and family members to describe your personality traits to you. This insight can be useful, since it's often hard for us to be truly objective about ourselves. Listen to what they have to say—and don't storm off in a huff if they say something you find hard to hear—use this insight to help you make decisions.

Chapter 7:
GROW RESILIENCE AND BOUNCE BACK

Buddhism

I was sat surrounded by sweaty, naked men, and it was all a bit awkward. I was also shaking like crazy—my entire body felt like it was buzzing and tingling with electricity. Definitely not your typical Tuesday morning ...

I had just been ice swimming in a frozen lake in Finland. And after getting incredibly cold and numb, I sprinted to the (already quite busy) lakeside sauna to escape the pain. I was grateful for the warmth, but my body went into convulsions due to the extreme temperature change. It was intense. My mind was in overdrive, telling me that this was good for me. Apparently ...

It is a Finnish tradition to jump into a frozen lake, swim until you can't handle the cold any longer, and then dash to the sauna to warm up. You do this several times until you feel amazing.

After a while, the endorphins kick in, and your body feels awesome.

But I won't lie: getting into a frozen lake is extremely painful. My brain was screaming at me to get out—it was a total primal survival response.

The mind plays a big role in this. Before I took the icy plunge, I watched two older Finnish women get in the freezing cold water as if it were a hot bath ... No big deal. They glided in, did a few laps, and looked at me as if to say: "We know what we're doing. Don't look so surprised. You'll get there one day." It was kind of inspiring and intimidating at the same time. When I finally mustered up the courage to get in the frigid, black water, it was ... a little more of a song and dance. I wasn't used to the pain; it was my first experience of ice swimming, and I had a lot to learn. Full disclosure: I made a lot of noise. Not so much Viking battle cries but more like a wheezy seal doing karaoke.

But here's the thing: when we challenge ourselves like this, we learn about our own minds and get a sense of how resilient we are. Life often throws us into situations that push our limits, so understanding how the mind works in extreme circumstances is valuable.

If you can convince yourself to get in an icy lake, having an awkward conversation with a friend feels like a breeze after that.

Well, in theory.

The term "resilience" has become synonymous with mental toughness. It's about how we handle adversity. How do we cope when life is intense, uncomfortable, and painful? What happens next? And how fast can we bounce back from challenges?

I used to have zero resilience and felt mentally weak a lot of the time. I would easily stress over little things like traffic jams, long lines, tangled wires, dropped toast, you name it. But over time, I've changed my response to these types of things. Doing stuff like ice swimming and tackling challenging situations has helped me to become mentally stronger. The more I pushed myself, the more resilient I became in general. Now, don't get me wrong: I still find some things tough. But compared to where I used to be, the progress is huge. And that's the key.

Resilience is not about being the toughest person on the planet; it's about making progress in your own life.

Can you handle things better than you used to? If so, that's progress. And it's awesome—good for you.

The great news is that anyone can develop their resilience. For me, the philosophical ideas from Buddhism have helped me cultivate a stronger mind—and they certainly helped me while I was neck-deep in that icy lake. So, let's take a deeper look at ...

Buddhism

Buddhism originated in northern India around the sixth century BCE and offers a clear method for building a resilient mind. It's profoundly powerful ancient wisdom and an incredibly practical system of self-development. Imagine it as a way to achieve inner peace, and get straight to the point of living a good life.

One of Buddhism's main goals is to help us handle the tough moments in life and suffer less. It's about dealing with both the physical and mental struggles with skill. According to some Buddhist teachings, the key to life is understanding how our minds work. How we frame our experiences has a huge impact on how we live. At the core of Buddhism lie the Four Noble Truths. Don't be fooled by the fancy name; it's a simple outline of how we can overcome suffering with mind training:

1. The truth of suffering: The first truth acknowledges the existence of suffering or dissatisfaction in life. If you're alive, you're going to suffer both physically and mentally. Sorry about that—but it's just part of the deal.

2. The cause of suffering: The real culprit behind our struggles is our own minds. Aha! I knew there had to be a root cause for all of this. It's like wanting things to be different, craving stuff, or being too attached to outcomes. Sound familiar?

3. The end of suffering: It's all good, though ... Don't worry. This truth offers hope by asserting that we can do something to overcome this suffering. If we can get our thinking straight, we're going to be OK. Good news.

4. The path that leads to the end of suffering: Through disciplined living and training the mind, we can transcend suffering. Enter **the Eightfold Path**—essentially a bunch of practical actions like meditating, being ethical, staying sober, being honest, spreading kindness, and promoting peace.

The Eightfold Path is crucial to the practice, and many Buddhists study it for a long time, but the main thing to remember is that Buddhism is largely about understanding our everyday reality.

There are approximately half a billion Buddhists around the world. The followers are typically split into two main branches of Buddhism: Theravada and Mahayana.

Theravada Buddhism is practiced in countries like Thailand and Sri Lanka, and it tends to follow the original teachings of Buddha, focusing on individual enlightenment. On the other hand, Mahayana Buddhism, found in places like China and Japan, embraces a bigger perspective, emphasizing compassion and the goal of helping all beings attain enlightenment.

These branches are further divided into various schools, leading to a diverse range of practices. Buddhism can therefore vary widely across countries and traditions.

Siddhārtha Gautama

Buddhism started with Siddhārtha Gautama, who lived in Northern India (now Nepal) somewhere between 600 and 400 BCE. He later became known as the Buddha after he achieved enlightenment, which is essentially an inner peace that comes from a deep understanding of life and the nature of suffering.

Siddhārtha's story goes like this: Siddhārtha was a prince who lived a privileged existence and had been protected from ever seeing old age, death, and disease. One day, Siddhārtha found himself outside the palace grounds and bumped into an old man. He started exploring more of life outside the palace and discovered disease and death. This challenged his entire worldview. He decided to leave the palace and his life of luxury behind, so that he could learn about transcending suffering. He headed off to the woods to meditate, train the mind, and try to understand the nature of reality. After years of effort, he achieved this goal, attained enlightenment, and became the Buddha—the "Enlightened one" or the "Awakened one."

After gaining a deep and profound understanding of the mind, Buddha began to share these ideas with others. His insights spread all over Asia and have evolved over time as they have mixed with different cultures and teachers.

Kisa Gotami

Pain, whether physical or mental, is part of life. Getting tougher doesn't mean dodging this pain but learning to embrace it. Realizing that life throws curveballs at us makes us better prepared. And once we accept this, we can gear up to tackle the tough times. The Buddhist story of Kisa Gotami (one of Buddha's most famous students) explains this perfectly:

Kisa was overrun with grief. Her only son had just died, and she was completely distraught. She visited the Buddha for help and asked him to bring her son back to life ... The Buddha replied that he would do this if she could first find some mustard seeds from a house that hadn't experienced death. After a long and desperate search, she realized that this was an impossible task. She returned unsuccessful.

Buddha explained that as mortals, we will all experience loss and death. It's part of life and something that everyone will encounter. This insight helped Kisa accept the nature of reality. Yes, it was still painful. But this acceptance allowed her to move forward through her grief. The story goes that this was the first step in her enlightenment process. She went on to study Buddhism, delving deeper into the philosophy.

Reducing Suffering

OK, we get that pain and suffering are inevitable and a natural part of life ... but what should we do when we encounter them? First, we don't want to add more suffering to the equation. We don't want to make things any worse—and our minds are definitely capable of doing this. This popular Buddhist parable explores this idea:

Imagine being shot with a poison arrow. You then go to a doctor who refuses to remove the arrow until they know more details. They want to know the origin of the arrow, who shot it, the reason you got shot, the type of poison, the brand of bow that was used, and the time of day the arrow was shot. All the while, poison continues leaking into your body as the doctor keeps asking questions. Yeah, that would be annoying, and you'd likely die if you didn't get the arrow removed ... You would be desperate for the doctor to deal with the problem without the overanalysis. Just take out the arrow, already!

Well, all of this represents our suffering in any given situation. If we're not careful, we can end up adding layer upon layer of problems to our original problem. Sometimes, we just need to get going with things and deal with the situation in front of us. Rather than getting caught up in the details of "Why is this happening to me?", we would be wise to focus on dealing with the problem at hand.

Everything Changes; Nothing Stays the Same

Buddhists believe that everything is in a state of flux and change. This is the idea of impermanence. Let's face it: nothing stays the same.

The concept of impermanence can help us become mentally tougher in many ways. It can work for boring, mentally painful situations like standing in line or sitting through a lesson you dislike. It can work for physical pain, such as broken bones, ice baths, and cuts and bruises. It can also work for mental pain based on fear and grief.

The power of knowing that nothing stays the same can be very helpful.

For instance, if you have to go to the dentist and are worried about it, focus on the short time frame. Think about the other side of the experience, and remind yourself that it won't last forever. Remembering that everything changes can be particularly helpful to hold on to.

If you are grappling with physical discomfort, consider redirecting your focus toward the future. Remind yourself that physical pain is transient and undergoes constant shifts. By closely observing the sensations of pain, you'll notice its fluctuating nature, moving from intense moments to dull phases and back again.

I always try to keep this in mind whenever I'm visiting the dentist ... It's a helpful coping strategy to have up your sleeve when needed.

Resilience Training

Buddhist monks will often do difficult things to train the mind and grow their resilience. From meditating to fasting to remaining silent for long periods of time, the idea of training is an important concept to them. The practices vary within different Buddhist communities and traditions, and some of these activities can be quite extreme:

- Tibetan Buddhist monks sometimes wrap themselves in wet sheets and sit outside in freezing temperatures. Using the power of the breath and the mind (a method known as "Tum-mo"), they can dry the sheets and not freeze to death.

- The marathon monks of Mount Hiei run 1,000 marathons in 1,000 days in straw shoes around the mountain tracks of northern Kyoto, Japan, as a way to build a mind of steel and achieve enlightenment. They aim to push the body and mind so far with the brutal nature of the task that they hope to reach enlightenment in the process.

- In Thailand, Buddhist monks have been known to meditate in a box of snakes. Sitting in a confined space, covered in pythons, trying to remain cool and not freak out, has got to be one of the ultimate tests of resilience.

All of these things are a way of training the mind. Yes, some of them are not exactly everyday to us, and we obviously don't need to commit to this kind of extreme task, but we can learn a lot from the philosophical concept of embracing difficulty as a way to develop a stronger mindset.

> "NO ONE SAVES US BUT OURSELVES. NO ONE CAN, AND NO ONE MAY. WE OURSELVES MUST WALK THE PATH."
>
> BUDDHA

Seriously Happy Hack

Life isn't always going to be easy. But if we can detach ourselves from overthinking and remember that nothing stays the same and everything changes, we can get better at managing suffering. We can also grow our resilience by learning to sit with uncomfortable situations that we have deliberately sought out.

The Challenges

Here are some practical ideas inspired by Buddhism that will help you boost your inner strength of character and help build your resilience and overall happiness.

1 Deliberate Discomfort

The first marathon I ran was brutal, and it hurt a lot. The 26-mile distance pushed me both physically and mentally, and I could barely speak afterward. It was definitely an exercise in managing suffering. At 20 miles, my brain started to plead with me: "I'm done. Whatever you're doing to me, I'd like you to stop. You don't have to finish this race!" Anyway, despite the internal racket, I managed to push through the barrier and complete the race. This mental hurdle is a very common experience when running a marathon—so much so that runners have nicknamed it "The Wall." No, it's not a physical barrier but a mental roadblock where you think you are done. But you're not; you just have to keep going to unlock the next level of grit within you. It's all about fostering that never-give-up attitude—the secret to growing your resilience.

A great way of connecting to this attitude is by becoming future-focused. This has helped me so much with all the marathons I've completed. Remembering the power of impermanence is key. Focusing on the fact that your pain will change at some point is crucial. Zoom out from the intensity of the moment, and push your mind into the future. Be assertive, stay strong, and show your mind that you are the boss of yourself.

For this challenge, your goal is to deliberately seek out mild physical discomfort, so that you can practice dealing with it. The more you learn to sit with physical discomfort, the better you get at managing those sensations.

Of course, please don't do anything crazy here. The key word is mild. I'm not talking about wild stunts. So, maybe don't copy the Tibetan monks by donning a wet sheet in subzero temperatures ...

Here are a few examples of things that you could actually try. Modify these based on what works best for you:

◎ Take a cold shower

Turn the faucet to cold, jump in, and see if you can stay in the shower for 30 seconds. Build it up over time, and you'll soon feel a natural boost of endorphins and increased tolerance to the cold.

◎ Complete a tough exercise routine

Push yourself to the limit with a workout that leaves you absolutely exhausted. This "positive exhaustion" is a sign that you're truly pushing your boundaries.

◎ Have a good stretch (challenging yoga poses are great for this)

Learn to sit with the mild discomfort that comes when you stretch your body. It will also be wonderful for increasing flexibility and preventing injuries in the future.

2   The Storm

Feeling overwhelmed by exams, an injury, or a school drama?
Draw a storm cloud (doesn't have to be perfect!), and mark your
progress with an X.

Visualize how much of the storm you've already weathered and
how much is left. As you move through it, keep moving the X.
Remember, like storms, difficult experiences pass—the Buddhist
concept of impermanence. Things will change and evolve. Hold
on to this.

3   Bored!

Turns out, boredom can be a mental gym! Here are some
surprisingly awesome ways to use those dull moments ... 😊:

- Listen to a song that you hate on repeat for an hour.
- Watch a movie from start to finish that you know is bad.
- Follow the second hand on a clock face for 20 minutes.
- Listen to the most boring podcast you can find.
- Line up for something, and then abandon the line at the
  last minute (this one is awful, sorry).

Learning to sit with mental discomfort and accepting it without
complaining is a real skill. And like all skills, it takes practice. So,
with that in mind ...

**Seek out mind-numbing activities, and turn them into
a test of your mental strength!**

Chapter 8:
FIND (SERIOUS) HAPPINESS!

Epicurus

My little boy was snuggled on my back in a carrier backpack making cute noises while my wife walked next to me holding my hand. The air carried the sweet yet earthy scent of the pine trees, and beyond them, an empty beach stretched along the vast blue-gray sea ahead. We followed a path leading to the sand, where the wind, tinged with the aroma of salt and seaweed, greeted us. The sky was blue, punctuated with cotton candy clouds and the occasional bird. It looked like a painting. Ready with snacks and drinks for an impromptu picnic, our day held no urgent plans and no work on the agenda. We had nothing to do but absorb ourselves in conversation and the world around us. In that moment, I was truly happy.

Moments of pure happiness and bliss like this are transient; they appear as fleeting pockets in time. Before you know it, you're back on the train (that's been delayed), and as you continue on, you spill hot coffee in your lap. Life is a roller coaster of highs and lows, yet we somehow forget this.

There is a common craving to be in a perpetual state of happiness, whatever that may mean—a relentless desire always to feel like everything is wonderful.

The pursuit of happiness has become an obsession that we collectively embrace. The United States Declaration of Independence states that "Life, Liberty and the pursuit of Happiness" are basic human rights. Happiness is portrayed as something to chase after, yet we often don't really know what it is. It's hard to define and will likely look different for each of us.

Moreover, happiness evolves over time. What might have made you happy as a child probably isn't the same as it is now. As we change, so do the things that make us feel happy. When I was little, I loved building dens in the woods. The bigger, the better. As a teenager, I loved going to gigs, playing video games, and roller skating. All these things made me happy at that point in my life. But again, that changed. I still love gigs but haven't been near roller skates for a long time.

While it's natural to wish for more happy times than not, the pursuit of happiness can become elusive and counterproductive. It's a little like organized fun: the desperation to have a "great" time can actually crush any genuine enjoyment. The desire to be happy at all times can lead us down a path of hedonism and overindulgence.

The constant battle to always feel good may ironically make us feel bad.

Imagine Nick, who is eagerly planning an epic weekend with friends. He meticulously schedules every moment, from gaming marathons to trying out new food spots, aiming to create the perfect collection of happy memories. However, as he stresses over making every moment extraordinary, the pressure to curate constant happiness becomes overwhelming. Meanwhile, his friend Sam, with no concrete plans, stumbles upon an outdoor concert where she discovers a new favorite band. The spontaneous, unexpected joy of the experience becomes a cherished memory, showing that happiness isn't always about planning every detail but letting the best moments happen naturally.

So, how do we genuinely become happier? What is happiness, and how do we keep it when we find it? And if it's not the end goal, then what is? Meet the remarkable Greek philosopher who can help us explore these questions. Hello, Epicurus. He has some fantastic ideas that will turn the conventional pursuit of happiness upside down, offering us plenty of insights that can contribute to a more satisfying life.

The Epic Epicurus

Born on the Greek island of Samos in 341 BCE, Epicurus was the philosopher behind Epicureanism, a philosophy centered on living the good life.

Epicurus believed that the meaning of life was to enjoy it. However, his legacy has been somewhat misinterpreted today. When people hear the term "epicurean," they often conjure images of lavish excess—maybe someone reclining while being fed grapes and simultaneously receiving a foot massage. This caricature reflects a common misunderstanding of Epicurus' message. His philosophy is not about extravagant indulgence, it's about finding joy in the simple things in life, avoiding unpleasantness, and connecting with others.

The Epicurean philosophy can teach us a lot about the simple art of happiness.

The Garden

Epicurus moved to Athens around 306 BCE and established a school called the Garden. Here friends would all happily hang out and live in a kind of small community. They would grow their own food—mainly fruit and vegetables—and would savor the fact that they had grown it themselves. The pleasure of knowing that they had produced it was all part of the fun. Generally, it was a slow pace of life that put a heavy emphasis on good conversations. Members were encouraged to shy away from politics and the public eye.

The school allowed women to live in the community and respected their opinions, which was revolutionary at the time. For many people in Athens, mixing males and females in this type of setting wasn't done. Epicurus didn't care. Nor did anyone else at the school. They just did what they wanted to do and didn't worry about what anyone else thought. Wild rumors about the school (mainly based on excessive eating and partying) were spread around the city, and this has most likely contributed toward the modern understanding of "epicurean" being synonymous with crazy parties of overindulgence.

One of the more famous women at the school was Leontion. There is an air of mystery around her, and we can't be entirely sure about the facts of her life—but we do know that Epicurus admired her greatly for her sharp mind. The fact that she was allowed to study reveals the inclusive nature of the Epicurean school, since both women and men were encouraged to study side by side—not a social norm of this time.

Leontion was said to be a great scholar who challenged Theophrastus, the head of the Lyceum, a rival philosophy school, by writing a comprehensive attack on his ideas. Her powerful arguments ruffled feathers, especially among male students. Sadly, her writings and full story are lost to time, leaving this intellectual firecracker something of a mystery.

The Simple Life

You'd be mistaken if you think rocking up to the Garden would mean partying late into the night. It was more like a modern-day community home than a party house. The food served was fairly uninspiring, consisting of basic fare like bread, homegrown fruits and vegetables, and boiled lentils. They also only typically drank water. Not the vision of Epicureanism you had in mind?

Yet, this simplicity was intentional and a central aim of Epicureanism. The idea was that by learning to appreciate the simple things, life could become less complicated, and you would be more content. Think about how deeply satisfying a simple glass of water tastes when you're really thirsty on a hot day. That's what the Epicureans were trying to cultivate with their minimalistic approach to living.

According to Epicureanism, an excess of anything is not going to make you happy. Too much of a good thing can become a bad thing; overeating can make you sick, excessive screen time hurts your eyes, and too much social media can leave you feeling brain-drained. Moderation is a key part of this philosophy.

Epicureans argued that excess leads to discomfort—basically, less is more! Overdoing anything leads to misery, just like a party that never ends. The initial fun fades, replaced by a desperate need to escape. Think about a big music festival ... By day three, it's all mud, mayhem, and the longing for a real bed. Moderation, as Epicurus advised, is the key to enjoying things for the long run.

Friends & Good Conversations

As a teenager, I played in a band, and we'd practice every Friday after school. It was an amazing way to kick-start the weekend. Sometimes our rehearsals were pointless, and it would just be about hanging out together.

We played lots of live gigs, and I loved doing this. My bandmate Jimi and I would usually climb onto my parents' shed roof after each gig to meticulously chat through the details of the performance. These are happy memories for me. You see, the time we spend with others is so important for our personal growth. There's an old saying that you are a mix of the five people you spend the most amount of time with ... so, pick wisely.

Cultivating good friendships is integral to our happiness and something that the Epicureans prioritized.

Conversation was an important part of life in the Garden. This was seen as one of the best ways to cultivate happiness. Having a good old chat and connecting with others was the secret ingredient for a good life. Discussing meaningful subjects like philosophy and the arts would be a common topic of choice. If you're considering joining this school of philosophy, simply brush up on your conversational skills, and you'll fit right in with the Epicurean life.

Removing "Bad Vibes"

For Epicurus, happiness meant kicking out negativity with a clear, calm mind. He saw knowledge and philosophy as tools to achieve this, using logic and reason, not just blind faith. He built on the work of earlier thinkers to create a practical approach to joy.

One major roadblock to a happy life, according to Epicurus, is the fear of death. He argued that this fear is irrational—death is inevitable for everyone. Instead of dwelling on it, Epicurus believed that accepting our mortality frees us up to truly enjoy the present.

Epicurus also felt that it was important to pull back from politics and public affairs—specifically, being ignorant of ongoing political scandals would make us much happier. Pulling away from news and social media could help get rid of some of the bad vibes ... News can be incredibly negative—sucking you in with sensational stories that are designed to keep you hooked. These days it's harder than ever to know what the truth is and unfortunately 'the news' is regularly a source of false information. Epicurus might tell you to skip it all.

Social media, on the other hand, can paint a very filtered picture of reality. Content based on "showing your best self" to the world has become increasingly prominent using filters, finding the perfect angle or highly editing videos. This helps breed "comparisonitis" and can make you compare your life less favorably to others.

However, it's just you can't see the whole picture of that other person's life to see their true ups and downs. Again, if Epicurus were here, he'd likely tell you to stay off social media.

YOLO

You know that the phrase "You only live once" or YOLO can often be used as an excuse for doing something stupid and potentially overindulgent. But how does this relate to Epicurus?

Well, if we follow this chain of thought, we might be able to connect the dots:

❀ Epicurus inspired the Roman poet Horace.

❀ Horace wrote the words "carpe diem" (or "seize the day") in one of his poems. (The saying obviously hit the right note and became popular in the modern world.)

❀ Well, YOLO is a little like this. It's essentially a slightly updated version of carpe diem.

❀ So, is Epicurus to blame? I guess ... a little ... for collectively getting people to focus on the pursuit of pleasure. But remember, Epicurus' pleasures were simple ones, and the avoidance of suffering also came into the equation. So, it's a kind of a misinterpreted version of his ideas. But whatever. Don't think about it too much. YOLO.

Epicurus was the real deal when it came to living his philosophy. He lived simply (walled garden, basic food), surrounded by friends and immersed in deep conversation and intellectual pursuits. His recipe for happiness? Less is truly more.

Some people worried that a philosophy based on pursuing personal happiness would lead to a selfish society. But if people prioritized their own happiness, this would make society a better place to be, surely? Just think about it. Imagine being surrounded by people who are genuinely happy. They are more likely to be kind, understanding, and supportive. Monday mornings at school might look very different.

Seriously Happy Hack

Learning to appreciate the simple things in life, cultivating good friendships, and removing ourselves from the turbulence of current affairs can help us live happy lives.

"BEING HAPPY IS KNOWING HOW TO BE CONTENT WITH LITTLE."
EPICURUS

The Challenges

Here are some ways to connect to Epicurus' ideas on happiness. The essence of Epicureanism is finding joy in simple pleasures and cultivating meaningful connections. You could tailor these challenges to your preferences and lifestyle—with the aim of embracing the philosophy to improve your well-being.

1 Simple Living

The goal here is to focus on appreciating the simple things in life. Food is a great way to test this.

◉ Why not tweak your meals a little and see what happens? Do you really need all that sauce? What's the simplest dish you can create for dinner? How about trying to savor the taste of very basic foods? Can you go without sugary treats? How long can you manage without chocolate? Can you avoid fast food?

Being conscious of your diet will benefit your physical and mental health and train your palate to appreciate fewer complex flavors.

◉ Challenge yourself to eat something ridiculously slowly, such as an apple in 10 minutes. Focus on every bite, savoring the flavors and smells. You might be surprised at how much more you appreciate your food.

It's all too easy to eat without thinking about what you're doing—the mind can be elsewhere, easily distracted by thoughts ... This slow-eating practice forces you to pay attention to the flavors in your mouth and helps you to savor the flavor—a slogan that would be fit for an Epicurean T-shirt.

2   Head in the Sand

No news. No social media. One week. Go.

Cutting out the negative news cycles and unrelenting social media feeds can help us disconnect from the intensity (and occasional insanity) of the world. The aim is to create space away from the noise of modern life and focus on living in the here and the now. Are you feeling happier yet?

I swear by digital fasts—a break from tech that boosts thinking and well-being. Sure, the first few days might be edgy, but then ... ah, the space! It feels like you gain hours (check your screen time, you'll be surprised). Disconnecting from the constant buzz is amazing. Try it—your mind (and body) will thank you.

3   H2Only

Ditch sugary drinks (coffee, tea, soda) for a week (or a month) and embrace plain water. Epicurus would be proud! Water complements every meal, and learning to love its pure taste reflects his philosophy perfectly.

Good job; your invite to Epicurus' Garden is in the mail.

Chapter 9:
RELATIONSHIP RESET

The Stoics (Again)

When I was learning to drive, my dad gave me a great piece of advice—he told me to assume that someone would try and crash into me every time I got in the car. I was shocked. What a strange thing to say, but it turns out that this was a good piece of advice. He taught me to overcompensate for other people's mistakes by expecting them to be sloppy on the road. Adopting this extra-vigilant attitude has helped me so much to become a better driver over the years—and helped me to avoid accidents.

I spent most of the time learning on quiet countryside roads. Sometimes, they were one-lane roads. Other times, they were backroads blocked by farm animals! It certainly kept me on my toes. But when I drove in the city, things were different. Horns honking, drivers and bikes cutting in, not giving way, traffic circles with a bazillion exits, and pedestrians crossing when they shouldn't. For someone who had learned to drive in a rural village, it felt chaotic. But thankfully, dad's advice came in handy—I was a lot more prepared for the chaos because I expected it to be there.

I've driven all over Europe, the United States, Australia, and New Zealand and have seen my fair share of wild driving. The reality is that, wherever you go, drivers can do unexpected things—drifting across lanes, sudden stopping, distracted and erratic driving. Unfortunately, accidents can happen, but dad's advice always encouraged me to make sure that I did something about the avoidable accidents and took control of what I could control. Stoic advice, indeed.

Much like driving, where unexpected encounters with sketchy drivers can test our patience and skills, life often thrusts us into contact with difficult people. Whether it's a chance encounter with a rude stranger, a peer, friend, or colleague who makes an unthinking remark, or someone who just really pushes our buttons, these encounters can be hard to handle. But the truth is, we all have to deal with these tricky experiences from time to time. Thankfully, there are ways for us to manage this ...

The Stoic philosophers recognized the inevitability of these "collisions" in life and gave us some wisdom on how to navigate them gracefully. Their advice for handling difficult people and situations is priceless—and, in many ways, incredibly similar to my dad's.

Stoicism (Again)

The Stoics again. Sorry, I couldn't help myself—there's just so much that we can learn from them. But this time, we'll look at a different aspect of the philosophy that combines kindness, preparation, and altering perceptions. So, let's start with that famous Roman ...

Marcus Aurelius is arguably the most well-known Stoic of all time.

He was the Roman Emperor from 161–180 CE and had a huge impact on popularizing Stoic philosophy. He used Stoicism throughout his reign as one of the most powerful people on the planet. It wasn't just a quaint set of principles for him; it was a tool he wielded to navigate wars, plagues, and personal tragedies. Marcus Aurelius had an incredibly difficult life and faced many hardships. It certainly wasn't an easy time to be an emperor.

Despite all this turbulence, he was known for being fair and kind. He sold the palace jewels to feed the poor. He made his brother co-emperor (which was unheard of). He gave gladiators wooden swords to reduce injury. And shock, horror, he actually lived by the law and followed the rules in place at the time. It would have been far too easy for him to be corrupted by all of that power, but because of these actions, he was loved by the citizens of Rome. In fact, he's still loved by a lot of people in the modern world.

Marcus wrote a book called *Meditations*, which has become one of the most important and widely read philosophy books of all time. The thing is, this was his diary and was never meant for publication. It was simply his way of reflecting on Stoic philosophy. Funny how, after his death, we're now reading his private journal and quoting it all over the Internet.

Marcus Aurelius' legacy lived on through his children, his reputation, and his book. His daughter, Annia Cornificia Faustina Minor, very much exemplified the Stoic way and followed his example. In later life, the emperor Caracalla assassinated her during a purge, but she faced her execution with dignity and self-control. Marcus' son Commodus, on the other hand, ended up being a bloodthirsty tyrant. He was the emperor who followed Marcus, but he was deeply mistrusted by many—quite the contrast to his father and sister.

One of Marcus' strengths was his ability to deal with difficult people. He believed that we should prepare in advance to meet these people.

At the start of each day, we should say to ourselves that we may well bump into people who challenge us.

Not all the time, of course, but we will encounter them in the world—this is simply a fact of life.

Thinking like this builds a picture of reality where we are prepared and not shocked if we meet someone unpleasant or difficult. This type of reframing is powerful. It allows us to prepare mentally.

It's very much like my dad's driving tip. By expecting a little erratic driving, we will be on the lookout and ready to respond mindfully. The same is true for challenging encounters with difficult people. If we know it might happen at some point, we can be more conscious about our response.

So, what do we do when these encounters happen? Well, the Stoics say that we should treat every negative encounter as a test of our character. We need to focus on our response to the situation. It's up to us to act accordingly, and Stoicism's Golden Rule of focusing on what we can control (see page 83) comes in here.

Are you in enough control of your mind to handle difficult people effectively? Can you be cool when a stranger is rude? When a friend makes a mean remark? Or when someone laughs in your face? The goal is to shift our focus toward how we deal with it. If we see the encounter as a challenge to be tackled, we will be better equipped to face it effectively.

THIS is the Stoic path.

TAKE A HOT MINUTE

There was a Stoic named Athenodorus Cananites who was the advisor to the Roman emperor Octavian. His tip for dealing with anger, particularly when responding to someone who had caused it, was to recite the alphabet before responding.

This is solid and timeless advice, like an ancient version of a "time-out." Creating a gap between stimulus and response allows us to take a hot minute. In haste, we can make mistakes, things can get broken, words get spoken that weren't meant to be said, and tempers can get out of control. We can learn a lot from this. If someone pushes your buttons, taking a minute to break away from the intensity of the situation can be helpful.

This is the Stoic response to handling difficult people.

Anti-Role Models

Another excellent Stoic-inspired way of viewing our encounters with difficult people is to think of them as teachers. The Stoics employed this technique and believed we could learn something useful from everyone. This attitude is empowering and turns a potentially negative encounter into something that has value.

In a way, we can see these tricky people as anti-role models. Essentially, through their actions and behavior, we can see how not to live and the paths in life to avoid. And the great news is that we don't need to dwell on this negativity. We can mentally thank our anti-role model teachers for this life lesson and then move on.

Kindness Wins

Building good relationships with others starts from a place of kindness—and being kind and cultivating a good character is integral to Stoic philosophy.

Stoicism encourages us to be good people and spread kindness, thereby making society and the world a better place to be a part of.

The famous Stoic Hierocles embodied this idea. He felt that our goal was to bring people closer to us through kindness. To treat strangers as if they were friends. To treat friends like they were family.

Hierocles' concept can be visualized as concentric circles: in the middle is YOU. The next circle is your family. Then friends. Then neighbors. Then people from your town. Then, your country. Then, everyone on the planet. The goal is to try and bring these circles closer to you and bring them toward the center.

PLANET
COUNTRY
TOWN
NEIGHBORS
FRIENDS
FAMILY
You

Marcus Aurelius talks about being kind, irrespective of who we encounter. It's then up to the other person to either be kind back or not, but either way, kindness is powerful, and it is magnetic. People will be more likely to want to work with you and want to spend time with you. So, to enhance your relationships with family, friends, peers, or strangers, start by being kind.

When we face difficult people and treat them with kindness, as hard as this might be, we are in a position of power. We aren't getting sucked into their ways of thinking and behaving. So, be like the Stoics and make kindness a priority.

Ubuntu & Sympatheia

A concept in Stoicism called "sympatheia" nicely relates back to kindness and the idea that together, we are greater than the sum of our parts. It's about the interconnected nature of humanity. We ARE humanity. Collectively, we make up the human experience. Marcus Aurelius puts it like this:

"What's bad for the hive is bad for the bee."

It's the idea that we are a part of society and that carries a responsibility. If we want the world to be a better place, then we need to live in a way that we would like others to live. We need to be good to each other, to prop each other up, and help society prosper.

The South African philosophical concept of ubuntu shares similarities with the Stoic idea of sympatheia. Both encourage us to look for our shared humanity—we are all connected. Nelson Mandela was well known for talking about ubuntu and exemplified this idea with how he handled the extreme racial tensions of apartheid in South Africa. His actions during this difficult time in history illustrate the strength that comes from being humanity-focused. One notable example is Mandela's commitment to reconciliation, as demonstrated through the Truth and Reconciliation Commission, a groundbreaking initiative to address past atrocities and foster national healing. Mandela was able to bring together a nation that was divided.

Unity is powerful, but division is a problem. The Stoics believe that we can find peace and make the world a better place when we come together. So, when we encounter conflict or difficult people, we would be wise to zoom out and focus on our shared humanity. Even small positive interactions can have a powerful ripple effect.

The Stoics have so much to say about life, and there's so much more for you to discover. Hopefully, you're convinced by now that the Stoics are a bunch of legends worthy of further exploration ...

To effectively deal with difficult people, Stoicism teaches us to be mentally prepared for unexpected encounters. Treat these situations as a test of character and respond with kindness.

"DOES SOMEONE DESPISE ME? THAT'S THEIR PROBLEM. MINE IS TO ENSURE THAT WHAT I DO OR SAY DOES NOT DESERVE SNEER. DOES SOMEONE HATE ME? AGAIN, IT IS THEIR PROBLEM. MY JOB IS TO BE FRIENDLY AND CHARITABLE TO EVERYONE, INCLUDING THOSE WHO HATE ME, AND SHOW THEM THEIR MISTAKE."

MARCUS AURELIUS

The Challenges

Here are some practical Stoic challenge ideas to help you be better prepared for dealing with difficult people.

1 Time Out

When I've given workshops to young people about philosophy, I often share the Stoic tip of not responding immediately to difficult people when angry, frustrated, or overly emotional.

This applies to many different situations that we all have to face. For example, if you reply to a text, email, or face-to-face comment when you're emotionally worked up, you can often end up saying something that you might later regret.

The Roman Stoic Seneca believed that the greatest remedy for anger was delay. By waiting and not leaning into anger, it would dissipate by itself. This advice is the same for when someone is the root cause of that anger; taking "time out" is a solid tactic. If possible, remove yourself from the immediate situation and get some space. Then, delay engaging with those powerful emotions. Athenodorus' alphabet trick (see page 136) can work well here, but sometimes you might need something a little more distracting.

I recommend finding a distraction like a number game, word puzzle, or chess app on your phone that can help activate the logical part of your brain.

Go for something that will fully engage you while you cool off.

I've used this when worked up, and it helps take the sting out of those emotions. Yes, it's a quick fix and might not solve the problem, but when you are more in control of your emotions, you will be better placed to work through whatever issue you are dealing with.

For this challenge, test the "time out" tactic when things get heated with difficult people. Put the idea into practice, and note what happens!

2 Entering the Dragon's Den

Deliberately seek out someone with a different point of view, and try to communicate with them in a measured way—don't lose your cool, or you lose the challenge. This is a real test of your mental control and is great training for dealing with hostility and difficult people in the real world. Stay kind and you win.

Try this with friends and family first—pick a spicy topic, and see if you can remain calm and in control when you encounter someone who thinks differently to you.

Some tips for good debating are:

- ◎ **Active listening**: This is where you *actually* listen to what the other person is saying. You acknowledge their point of view and give them the space they need to express themselves.

- ◎ **Responding with empathy**: Here, you focus on being kind with your response and tone.

- ◎ **Staying calm**: When talking about heated topics, it's easy to get caught up in anger and frustration. The goal is to stay calm whatever happens, since this puts you in a position of power. If you lose control, you can end up saying things you regret.

- ◎ **Know when to call it a day:** If you face a stalemate and no one is willing to change their mind, it's important to know when or how to effectively change the topic and move on.

You could also explore this further by observing online debates on social media. It's easy to spot someone who has stoic self-control here and is working from a place of kindness and respect. Having said that, you might not want to spend a lot of time doing this. Social media and the online world can be great, but there is also a darker side. Luckily, you've been paying attention to Marcus Aurelius and know that things like this can happen. So, you're ahead of the game. You just move on and remain calm and in control.

Chapter 10:
LEVEL UP YOUR DISCIPLINE

A Mix of Ancient Philosophies

Albert Lee's *Country Boy* is a brutally fast song with an unrelenting lead guitar part. This Country Rock classic has become a real benchmark for advanced guitar players to test their skills. It's eye-wateringly hard. The guitar part is technical, incredibly quick, and filled with awkward hand positions. It took me hours of practice to learn this song on the guitar, and even then, it sounded a bit sketchy. When I thought I had it down, I'd check in with the record and realize that it was even faster than I had been practicing.

Endless rehearsals, patient bandmates, and finally ... perfection! It took intense effort and practice to turn the "impossible" into "nailed it." That is the power of discipline and self-control—a lesson I will never forget.

Whether it's been writing books, climbing mountains, running marathons, learning the Rubik's cube, speaking to audiences, or playing guitar, I find that the greater the challenge and the greater the effort required to get there, the greater the sense of achievement has been. It's through this determination and effort that we experience a sense of reward.

Committing to a goal and sticking with it long enough to see results is the best way to connect to the life-changing power of discipline.

Yes, it can be hard to keep going sometimes, and there have certainly been moments in my life when I felt like I wanted to quit (this tends to happen when I'm WAY out of my comfort zone). But working through the resistance and leaning into discipline helps me to face those obstacles. Ultimately, discipline and self-control empower us to steer our thoughts in the right direction. It's about showing our brains who's in charge, and once we master that, we can achieve amazing things.

Discipline isn't just a tool; it can set you free.

It will keep you moving forward and help you progress in anything you choose to do. Whatever you're aiming for in life, discipline and self-control can pave the way.

Discipline is a common theme throughout all of the philosophies in this book; in a way, it ties them together. And since this is the final chapter, we're going to be doing things a little bit differently … Rather than look at a specific school of philosophy, we're going to look at them all together. Since they all share discipline as a common thread, it felt right to invite everyone to the party.

Philosophy in the Mix!

The ancient philosophies featured in this book—Zen, Cynicism, Taoism, Stoicism, Aristotelianism, Buddhism, the Socratic School, and Epicureanism—all value discipline very highly.

There are two main ways that we can see this:

- ◎ **Words**—Lots of these philosophies directly talk about how important it is to live a disciplined life. The power of self-control and moderation is a common theme.

- ◎ **Actions**—The way the philosophers lived their lives gives us a great insight into their daily discipline. The fact that many of these philosophers were in top physical condition and wrote prolifically, publishing dozens of books and articles, is evidence of this. We can also see it in their commitment to practices like Tai Chi, meditation, and askesis (mental toughness training).

Let's dive in a little deeper and explore both aspects.

Word Up

Discipline is a topic beloved by many philosophers. We'll start with one of the most famous ones: Plato. When you think about philosophy, his name will usually be near the top of the list, right?

Plato was Socrates' most well-known student and created the world's first university, The Academy, in Athens in 387 BCE. He was also a top-class wrestler with a muscular physique. Yes, Plato was shredded and poised to instill philosophy into anyone who would listen.

In Plato's most famous book, *Republic*, we learn about his "cardinal virtues."

147

These are the core values that he believed we should all live by:

- ◉ wisdom
- ◉ justice
- ◉ courage
- ◉ moderation or temperance.

Now, out of these virtues, moderation or temperance is particularly relevant because it concerns discipline and self-control—a quality of character highly valued by the ancient Greeks.

Moderation or temperance refers to the practice of finding balance and avoiding excess in one's actions, emotions, or desires.

It's the art of exercising restraint and maintaining a measured approach to life, aligning perfectly with the theme of discipline and self-mastery.

Because Plato was such a big thinker in the world of philosophy, his thoughts on discipline, moderation, and temperance have spread across the world. When Plato spoke, people listened, and this meant that discipline was valued by many who followed him. Aristotle, Plato's most notable student, showed us how important self-control and discipline were to him with his Golden Mean (see page 98), an idea based on finding the perfect amount of virtue in any given situation.

Epicurus advocates embracing moderation and not overdoing it. The Stoics talk a lot about self-control. And the Cynics, well, they pretty much wrote the handbook for self-sufficiency and living a disciplined life.

In parallel to this, if we look at Buddhism, we'll also find a heavy emphasis on discipline. In fact, there's a concept called "the Middle Way," which is another way of saying "to live a disciplined life." This is all about living a balanced lifestyle, maintaining moderation, and staying in control. The Eightfold Path is also a series of practical actions that many Buddhists follow. Discipline is integral to this philosophy.

Actions Speak Louder?

We also see how important discipline was to a lot of philosophers by their actions—many of them started schools and taught their ideas to countless students, such as Chiyono, the Zen monk who established the first female Rinzai Zen school in Kyoto.

Others disappeared into solitude to practice meditation and asceticism (the practice of extreme fasting and general deprivation). This was one of the key things that the Buddha did on his journey to enlightenment, although he later realized that he had taken his asceticism too far and it became detrimental to his philosophical progress.

The Cynic philosopher Hipparchia was another amazing example of discipline in action—specifically in the way she embraced discomfort (and encouraged her children to do the same!) by taking cold baths and eating very simple food.

Thankfully, a lot of these philosophers committed to sharing their wisdom through their books. The process of writing a book is an act of discipline in itself, so we get a glimpse into the committed mindsets of many of these philosophers. Chrysippus, the third head of the Stoic school, wrote more than 700 books. Unfortunately, all are now lost.

But for me, one of the best places to observe discipline in action is when these philosophies encourage the development of a specific practice. Taoism has Tai Chi and Qigong. Stoicism and Cynicism have mental toughness training (askesis). Zen has meditation. Buddhism has the Eightfold Path. Epicureanism has an appreciation of simple food. All these practices allow the philosophy to be put to the test in a very tangible way through specific actions. The fact that so many ancient philosophers practiced these actions tells us how important they were to understanding the philosophies.

STRIKE A (YOGA) POSE

Yoga, with its roots in ancient Indian philosophy, goes beyond physical postures. It's a practice combining physical challenge and self-discipline to explore deeper ideas about ourselves and the universe. From breath work-focused Kundalini to partner acroyoga, various styles have emerged, all rooted in this 5,000-year-old philosophy. Another perfect example of philosophy in practice.

In Zen, there's an expression:

From one thing, know ten thousand things.

And this is where the power of getting good at a particular practice, whether that's mastering yoga poses, video games, or the guitar, comes into play. When we become good at something through practice, we learn philosophical lessons about discipline. We learn about effort versus results. We learn about working through setbacks and plateaus. And we learn about balancing life around our commitments.

Obviously, we don't have to engage in the same practices the ancient philosophers were doing (meditation, Tai Chi, askesis, etc.) Any activity—sports, music, even languages—can teach you about yourself and the world. Just as my guitar journey boosted my philosophy knowledge, any passion can hold hidden lessons.

Blue Train

While writing this book, one album has been on repeat in the background: *Blue Train* by John Coltrane. I've listened to this album possibly more than any other in my life. I now associate creativity with this music, and so when I hear Coltrane play the saxophone, it gets me into "the zone."

Coltrane was an influential American Jazz saxophonist and composer during the 1950s and 1960s, and he exemplified discipline in his life. A lot of people claimed that he wasn't naturally gifted on the sax, but he compensated for this by becoming the hardest-working person in the room. He practiced so much that he literally became one of the best musicians in the world. A famous quip was that he practiced 25 hours a day. Coltrane was also known to fall asleep with the sax in his mouth—because he was always practicing.

At the height of his career in the late 1950s and early 1960s, he recorded many notable albums with the Blue Note record label and collaborated with some of the best musicians on the planet. He is regarded as one of the greatest jazz musicians of all time. Although not a philosopher, his unrelenting commitment to his craft and his intense self-control illustrate the dazzling power of having a disciplined mindset.

Incredible things happen when you commit to your dreams.

Get into the Routine

I learned about the power of a morning and evening routine from the Stoics, who loved to start and finish the day with structure. This is a fantastic way to welcome discipline into your life.

The Stoic philosopher Seneca usually did some exercise in the morning. A cold bath would typically follow this. Then maybe some simple food for breakfast. He would finish the day by looking back over what had happened to him. He was careful to learn from whatever he had encountered—a testament to his very self-reflective attitude. The other well-known Stoics, Epictetus and Marcus Aurelius, also made space for reflecting in the evenings. In modern Stoic circles, it's become a common practice to journal at the end of the day. I was inspired by these ideas and began structuring my mornings and evenings several years ago.

It had a profound impact on my life and has helped me to become more productive.

A typical morning routine for me includes exercise, meditation, and a cold shower. The routine does change over time, so it won't always look like this. I used to wake up incredibly early to do it, but these days, I prioritize sleep more than I used to. However, I still like to start the day strong and know what a positive impact it can have on me.

I also try to close the day with an evening routine. This is likely to be a spot of journaling and reading—nothing crazy here. It's supposed to be a chilled way to end the day. I try to avoid going on my phone right before I go to sleep, so I normally choose to wind down with a book.

Keeping to this routine takes discipline and is a great way to ensure that my mind is strong.

Many philosophers had strong routines in general (not just the morning and evening combination). Simone de Beauvoir (a famous Existentialist philosopher in the twentieth century) built a routine that allowed her to write in the morning, meet friends at lunchtime, and then write again in the afternoon. She was incredibly disciplined about this, which made her phenomenally productive. Over the years, her contribution to philosophy has been enormous by helping to grow feminist philosophy, fighting for equality, and encouraging people to embrace freedom. Her legendary status is part and parcel of the disciplined routine she followed.

Discipline is powerful. It's a recurring theme in the philosophies we've covered, and the fact that such a broad spread of philosophers used discipline in their daily lives indicates the universal strength it holds. So, start building your discipline powers today!

Seriously Happy Hack

The ancient philosophers throughout this book understood the power of self-control, commitment, and discipline. By bringing these ideas into our lives, we can achieve incredible things.

The Challenges

Let's do some activities to help you become more disciplined. These will boost your productivity, improve self-control and flex your powers of perseverance.

1 Morning & Night

Choose a morning/evening routine from below, and stick with it. Don't sweat slipups, just start again the next day. Use a calendar or app to track progress and visualize your commitment.

Morning/evening routine ideas:

- meditation
- journaling
- cold shower
- reading
- exercise
- walk in fresh air
- make your bed
- warm bath
- breath work
- learning a new skill.

2 Resist

Do you have the self-control and discipline of mind to say no? If you can resist the temptations around you, even when your brain is trying to convince you otherwise, you'll know that you are the one running the show—not your base instincts and primal mind. The mind I'm talking about is the mind that wants to eat ice cream every day. The mind that wants to eat ALL of the chocolates. The mind that wants to laze in front of the TV on the sofa and drink soda all day. The mind that never wants to get out of bed.

Well, how much does your mind control you? Let's find out ...

For this challenge, take a tiny bite of a chocolate bar, and then see if you can fight the urge to eat the whole thing.

1. Get hold of your favorite chocolate bar.

2. Unwrap it, and spend time smelling the chocolatey aroma.

3. Take a tiny bite of the chocolate.

4. Put the bar down, and resist the temptation to finish the whole thing.

5. Pay attention to the magnetic pull toward the chocolate— notice this sensation, but don't give in!

For anyone who likes chocolate, this is incredibly hard. However, if you don't have a sweet tooth, and the chocolate challenge is too easy for you, replace chocolate with something else that you really enjoy and practice resisting that instead. Bon appétit.

3 Philosophical Practices, AKA Your New Hobby

Bring philosophy into your life by picking one of the practices mentioned in this book and use it on a regular basis. Try them all out first to see which one you connect with the most, and then commit to going deeper with one of them. See how far you can take it with regular effort. Can you do one of these things for an entire year? Not only will it grow your discipline muscles, but it will also help you to get closer to the philosophy connected to it. Here's a reminder of the practices you could explore:

- ◎ Qigong
- ◎ Tai Chi
- ◎ meditation
- ◎ askesis training
- ◎ yoga.

I try to use all of them in my life regularly but find that meditation and askesis training are my preferences.

A good way to introduce one of these practices into your life is by carving out regular time in your day to learn about one that interests you. Use this space to immerse yourself in the practice. There are so many free online resources to get you started.

Good luck on your journey to a disciplined mind!

Part 3

CONCLUSION

Think Like a Philosopher

Well, that was a whirlwind tour of philosophy. I hope some ideas resonated with you and sparked your curiosity for further exploration. There's a lot to take in, but my main suggestion is to test the ideas in the real world since ...

philosophy comes alive when you apply its ideas in your daily life.

Experiment and see what works for you.

Honestly, it doesn't matter where you start, whether it's with your decision-making, confidence, focus, or resilience. Just begin using the ideas, and you will soon feel how powerful they are. These lessons can be life-changing.

If you don't know how to get the ball rolling, start with the challenges at the end of each chapter. These are fantastic ways to connect to the ideas from the philosophies. Rope in your friends, have fun, and keep an open mind.

A Better You

The goal of all this philosophy is ultimately to build good character, live up to our potential, and grow as human beings. This, in turn, helps us feel happier and better prepared for the world's chaos.

Philosophers and thinkers throughout history highly valued this approach to life, as can be seen by their heavy emphasis on living a virtuous life throughout their writings and teachings.

There's a concept called "arete" that comes from ancient Greek philosophy and is particularly relevant here. I learned about it from the Stoics and absolutely love it.

Essentially, "arete" means always trying to be your best self in every situation.

Of course, this is an ongoing process and something that we need to keep working on—we're unlikely to be our best selves ALL the time. None of us are perfect. We can be crabby and make mistakes. Doors get slammed. Rude comments get made. Horns get honked. Bad habits float to the surface ... But what matters is what we do next. Can we dust ourselves off and keep going? Do we move forward and continue tweaking our behavior? It's this striving to be better that is so important. This is arete to a tee.

Now, WHY does this matter? Well, when you start to upgrade your character with the philosophical ideas in this book, you'll face some hurdles along the way. Trust me. Even these powerful ideas require consistent practice. It's an ongoing process of self-improvement, and when you learn to enjoy that process, things become easier. You'll become less hard on yourself when you slip up. You know that it's all part of the journey, and progress isn't always a straight line.

THE HAPPINESS EQUATION

Finding a nice balance between building your character and being happy with where you are in life is important. Yes, it's a little bit of a paradox to be content but also want more. Driven yet satisfied does seem like a contradiction.

However, I believe that you can achieve this balance with the right mindset. If we can hold both concepts in our heads, we can have a more holistic approach to our overall happiness. I think about it like an equation:

Self-acceptance and gratitude

Self-improvement and living up to your potential

 Happiness

Hopes for Humanity

I have incredibly high hopes for the future and am genuinely excited by what's around the corner. There are just so many wonderful things happening in the world. Yes, we are very far from everything being perfect, and I know that there are a lot of serious challenges ahead. But I am choosing to look on the bright side, staying optimistic about the incredible things happening on this beautiful planet and striving for a more equal distribution of happiness.

Socrates said: "The secret of change is to focus all of your energy, not on fighting the old, but on building the new."

He meant that, as we encounter change, we should shift our focus to what we can do to make a difference. What will actually help all of us? This applies to the world around us and also on an individual level.

Inspired by this quote, and philosophically speaking, there are two fantastic ways that we can help to make the world a better place:

1. Start with you

To make the world better, start with yourself. Your actions have a ripple effect on countless lives. Every interaction matters, and you contribute to a happier humanity by being a decent person. We start that domino effect by working on living a virtuous life and cultivating a good character.

2. Innovate

As the saying goes: "If you always do what you've always done, you'll always get what you've always got." And a lot of the things we're doing in the modern world aren't working, let's admit that. This is where we come in. To create meaningful change, we should focus on innovation—and this comes from asking questions, thinking outside the box, and being open-minded. In other words, thinking like a philosopher.

You can innovate in many ways:

- ◎ bringing people together
- ◎ challenging things that aren't working within society
- ◎ not being afraid to ask difficult questions
- ◎ sharing your observations
- ◎ inventing new solutions to old problems.

One revolutionary idea can spark a global shift. Open your mind, focus on creative solutions, and your impact could rewrite the world's story.

The world needs movers and shakers.

The world needs more philosophers.

Philosophy empowers us, both individually and together, to build a brighter future. I believe its wisdom holds immense potential to change the world for the better.

Seriously Happy?

Inevitably, writing a book with happiness as its core message means that I should discuss my relationship with happiness. I touched on this earlier, but there's more to say on the matter.

Philosophy isn't a magic bullet for constant happiness. Life throws curveballs, and sometimes sadness or grief are the natural responses. But philosophy equips us to navigate this emotional roller coaster. We learn to savor the good times and find strength during the lows, knowing that things will eventually shift. It's about resilience, not chasing fleeting joy.

All storms pass. So do all rainbows. Everything is temporary.

This is why I resonate so deeply with the philosophy of eudaemonia. It's a broader sense of fulfillment that goes beyond fleeting happiness. It's about growth, resilience, and finding meaning in life. In fact, this concept has inspired me a lot and helped me to really question what is important to me. Eudaemonia feels like something I can work toward, irrespective of what is happening in my life. I don't need to look outside of myself for this. It's more of an internal quest than pursuing a specific object or moment. It's more about the journey than the destination. So, cheers to the wild ride!

Final Thoughts

I'd like to end this book by thanking you for coming on this journey with me. I appreciate you being here and hope these ideas make a difference in your life.

I wish you two things: a strong mind to endure tough times and a present mind to enjoy good times.

Life is a beautiful gift, and I hope you find serious happiness along the way.

"VERY LITTLE IS NEEDED
TO MAKE A HAPPY LIFE;
IT IS ALL WITHIN YOURSELF,
IN YOUR WAY OF THINKING."
MARCUS AURELIUS

Reading Recommendations

Explore further! This book is just the tip of the iceberg. Follow the ideas that spark your curiosity: there's a path for everyone. Here are some of my favorite philosophy books and references that I used in my writing to get you started.

Zen

What is Zen?—**Alan Watts**—New World Library, 2000
A fantastic introduction to Zen by the legendary Alan Watts.

Everyday Zen—**Charlotte Joko Beck**—Thorsons, 1996
A beautiful exploration of Zen and meditation.

Hardcore Zen—**Brad Warner**—Wisdom Publications, 2016
A unique take on Zen with punk rock, monsters, and a Zen monk's journey.

Stoicism

Meditations—**Marcus Aurelius**—Random House Publishing Group, 2003
One of my favorite philosophy books of all time. This is one of the key texts of Stoic philosophy.

Discourses and Selected Writings—**Epictetus**—Penguin Classics, 2008
Bite-size Stoic wisdom, like ancient blog posts.

Letters from a Stoic—**Seneca**—Penguin Classics, 2004
A Stoic buddy's advice in letters, tackling various issues.

How to Control the Uncontrollable—**Ben Aldridge**—Welbeck Balance, 2022
My Stoicism book!

A Guide to the Good Life—**William B. Irvine**—OUP USA, 2009
My favorite Stoic overview, a must-read.

Cynicism

The Cynic Philosophers from Diogenes to Julian—**Robert Dobbin**—
Penguin Classics, 2012
An essential book for anyone interested in Cynicism—highly recommend

Aristotle

***Aristotle's Way*—Edith Hall**—Vintage, 2019
A deep dive into Aristotle's life and work by a fantastic writer.

***Nicomachean Ethics*—Aristotle**—Penguin Classics, 2020
Start here for an intro to Aristotle's ideas.

Socrates

***The Last Days of Socrates*—Plato**—Penguin Classics, 2003
An essential read packed with stories about Socrates.

***The Socratic Method*—Ward Farnsworth**—David R. Godine, Publisher, 2021
A solid overview of Socrates' philosophy in action.

Buddhism

***The Dhammapada*—Eknath Easwaran**—Nilgiri Press, 2007
A must-read translation of a classic Buddhist text.

***Why Buddhism Is True*—Robert Wright**—Simon & Schuster, 2018
My favorite! Explores Buddhism from a psychological perspective.

***Buddhism Plain and Simple*—Steve Hagen**—Penguin, 1999
A wonderful intro to Buddhist ideas, beautifully written.

Taoism

***Tao Te Ching*—Lao-tzu**—Penguin Classics, 2003
The most profound and beautiful Taoist classic, perfect with a cup of tea.

***The Book of Chuang Tzu*—Chuang Tzu**—Penguin Classics, 2006
An entertaining classic with stories and humor.

***The Tao of Pooh*—Benjamin Hoff**—Farshore, 2018
This explains Taoism through Winnie the Pooh (strangely amazing!).

***The Te of Piglet*—Benjamin Hoff**—Egmont, 2019
An excellent follow-up to *The Tao of Pooh*, also highly recommend.

Epicurus

The Art of Happiness—**Epicurus**—Penguin Classics, 2013
A great selection of writings from Epicurus and other Epicureans.

Travels with Epicurus—**Daniel Klein**—Oneworld Publications, 2014
A witty and wise look at aging through an Epicurean lens.

General

The Philosopher Queens—**Rebecca Buxton and Lisa Whiting**—Unbound, 2020
This explores the contributions of women philosophers.

Plato and a Platypus Walk into a Bar—**Thomas Cathcart and Daniel Klein**—Penguin Books, 2008
Hilarious intro to philosophy through jokes.

Sophie's World—**Jostein Gaarder**—Weidenfeld & Nicolson, 2015
A captivating novel that teaches philosophy history.

History of Western Philosophy—**Bertrand Russell**—Routledge, 2004
A comprehensive guide to Western philosophy (beware, it's a brick!).

Lives of the Eminent Philosophers—**Diogenes Laertius**—Oxford University Press, 2020
Ancient biographies of philosophers—a classic primary source.

Audio Lectures—**Alan Watts**—www.alanwatts.org
Listen to the iconic voice of Alan Watts for an intro to Eastern philosophy (not a book, but a great resource!).

www.nami.org
If you are concerned about your mental health, this website is a great way to access professional help and advice. It has lots of useful resources and practical information. I would always recommend getting professional help if you feel overwhelmed and worried about your mental health.

Want more? See my website for ridiculous philosophy adventures (and social media, unless you're on an Epicurean digital detox!).
www.benaldridge.com

Acknowledgments

I'd like to thank the following people for helping me with this project:

My wonderful publisher—Quarto. I've had the pleasure of collaborating with so many incredible people while working on this book. Thank you to everyone who has been part of this journey. I really appreciate everything that you do.

Robert Gwyn Palmer has been an amazing support over the years. I'm very lucky to have such a kind, wise, and knowledgeable agent in my corner.

Debbie Foy had a profound impact on this book—she made all of this possible! I've adored working with her and feel unbelievably grateful for her input and support. She has taught me so much.

Harriet Birkinshaw has been a fantastic editor to collaborate with on this book. I'm so thankful for all of her insightful advice and feedback.

Holly Edgar also helped to keep my thinking clear and has been a very supportive editor.

Michelle Brackenborough's design and illustrations have turned my words into a beautiful book. I'm so grateful for all of her hard work on this, and I think the end result looks absolutely fantastic!

Special thanks go to my mum and dad for helping with this book in countless ways—from reading drafts to chatting through ideas; I'm very grateful for their help.

And then we have Helen and Oli. My world. Thank you both for being patient with me while I worked on this project. Helen—your support has been incredible. You've always been there for me and I couldn't have done this without you. Oli—you're a total inspiration and the main reason I've wanted to write for a younger audience. I hope that you enjoy this book when you're old enough to read it. I love you both.

And finally, I'd like to thank you, dear reader. Thank you for being here. By reading my work, you help me to realize my dream of being a writer. I appreciate you.